I0630900

Billionaire Protector

Billionaire Series

J.L. Ryan

Published by J.L. Ryan, 2018.

BILLIONAIRE PROTECTOR

First edition. June 1, 2018.

Copyright © 2018 J.L. Ryan.

ISBN: 978-1393556619

Written by J.L. Ryan.

Bad Boy Alphas

A Bad Boy Alpha Billionaire Romance Series

The Billionaire's Wish

Braden Davenport was on cloud nine. Even now, as he pulled off his helmet, he felt great. He was on a streak and this was going to be his best season yet. He brushed his hand through his jet-black hair and smiled at the people around him. It was nice having fans. They were the only constant in his life, always there to cheer him on. The problem was, they didn't really know him.

That's not to say that it isn't great doing what you love for a living. He was able to buy his first house at the age of 23, and at 29, he owned three. He liked to have a nice place to stay whenever he was in his favorite places. Racing was a dangerous sport, but it was in his blood, a part of him. Being here in Austin for the MotoGP race had been a fluke, but a happy one. He was a last minute add in and he was happy he said yes.

He would always rather be racing than home alone or out with some nameless girl that didn't know him very well. For now, he was home in Texas, at least for the next two months. It was the place where this all began and he was happy to be there. He loved the dry air and the open grounds in the hill country, and the city life in Austin. His next race was in Vegas and he was happy for the break. The win today would put enough money in the bank that he could live off forever, but it was never enough. Having lived such a hard life growing up, he liked the better, secure, lifestyle he had now.

He basically lived his life in an orphanage. He never knew his father, who left his mother soon after he was born. His mother was heartbroken and soon became an addict. He still remembered what it was like finding her there when he was 7. She made the wrong person mad, and they gave her some bad stuff. He found her unresponsive, lying on the living room floor. They didn't have a phone, but fortunately he was able to run to a neighbor and they called the police for him. He still carried around the guilt because he couldn't save her.

He eventually left the orphanage and made a few friends. He had a difficult time trusting people, getting close to anyone.

He got his first job at the thrift store in town. He learned the hard way that life was about making the right choices or you end up with nothing. Over time, he managed to secure a room, and that's when he met Gerald and Abbie Smith. Older, they were frequent shoppers where he worked, and they always amused him. At 80, Gerald was a big bear of a man. Abbie was a tiny little thing at 77. Abbie would tell Braden he looked too thin, and Gerald would pull him aside and talk cars with him, something he always loved. After a year or so, they invited him to dinner. At 19, he still seemed like a kid to Abbie. She was always fussing over him and making sure he actually ate when he came over.

Gerald was the person who taught Braden to race. He owned many bikes, he was a collector of sorts, and the moment Braden rode one, his life changed. He maneuvered them like a pro. After some help from Gerald's contacts, he quickly became successful and was able to secure himself a lucrative future in racing. When Braden was 21, Gerald passed away, and Abbie followed a year later. He moved in to help her after Gerald's passing, and held her hand when she died.

That was seven years ago now, and he could still remember it like it was yesterday. He shook his head, remembering, and smiled. He made sure his bike was always in tip top shape, and made frequent visits to his trusted mechanic and best friend, Mike's house. They met in his early years of racing, and had been friends ever since.

The most important thing that Gerald taught Braden was that the bike is your money and the only way you can ride it safely is if you have a hand in what goes on with it. The bike was his family, and he protected it as such. He finally set off for the hour drive to Marble Falls, where Mike lived.

Mike was always a party guy. One girl to the next and one disaster away from an addiction. What he did have was a nice house, and a

serious garage behind it. It was the one thing he always took care of.
His mother would come over once a month and clean up for him. As
he pulled into the parking lot of the townhouses, Braden noticed the
changes. The place next door was vacant the last time he was there, and
he wondered if Mike even knew that someone had moved in.

He was taking the next few weeks to run off with his newest
girlfriend and had given Braden the key so that he could drop some
things off, and pick up some things for the bike. He noticed her the
moment he pulled up. He watched amused as a woman was desperately
trying to get her key to work in her door knob.

"Damn it."

She was angry and she was beautiful. She finally kicked the door
and turned to go to her car. She stopped when she saw him watching
her. She gave him a half smile before pushing her hair back and squaring
her shoulder.

"I'm not usually so easily flustered. My key broke off in the door...
now I am rambling sorry... so yeah, I should go." She turned to go again
and he finally said something.

"I can probably get that out of there if you want me to try."
He crossed his arms as she gave him a half smile.

"That would be... well... yes, please." She smiled at him again
and he went to the truck.

Chloe closed her eyes and took a deep breath. She was standing
here rambling like an idiot. It always happened when she met a guy,
especially an attractive one. Attractive didn't even begin to describe this
one. He was, by far, the most attractive guy she had seen in a long time.
He had black hair and dark eyes and just enough stubble on his face to
give him that mysterious look. She never even kissed a guy like that and
she never would. It certainly didn't hurt to watch him though. He was
all muscle, and it was obvious he worked out. She blushed as he came

back towards her, hopefully he hadn't seen her looking him over like that.

He smiled as he worked on the door. She was looking him over and it made him smile. The fact that she blushed when he looked at her made him like her even more. He finally broke the broken key out and he turned to look at her again. It was her eyes that struck him first. Deep blue and full of life, they contrasted the abundance of red flowing hair. She was a big girl, he liked that about her. She had curves in all of the right placed and he wanted to touch every single one of them. He glanced at her hand and didn't see a ring, which was a good first step. He handed her the broken pieces of the key, and when his eyes met hers, he saw her blush again.

"It should be fine now, I had to put some lube in it." He gave her a half smile.

"What... oh thanks." She gathered the pieces up and headed towards the door. "Thanks again..."

"Braden... my name is Braden." He held his hand out to her and she shook it.

"I'm Chloe, nice to meet you."

"Perhaps I can get you to have dinner with me sometime, Chloe?" He watched the myriad of emotions cross her face.

"Sure, that sounds like fun." She turned to head back in again and he smiled.

"Chloe, can I get your number?"

"Oh, sorry." She wrote it down and turned to go again.

She was a flighty one, but that was part of the excitement for him. He watched her go inside and he left, heading for his place in the hills. She was timid, something he would remedy. Even now he thought about her curves and how they would feel under his fingers. He rarely ever lost at this and he didn't intend to start now.

Chloe shut the door with a thud. That was very sweet of him, offering to have dinner with him. It was typical of some guys, nicer ones anyway, to offer to take the big girl out. She didn't need to get paraded around and everyone's opinion of him go up because he did her a favor. Still, he seemed genuine. She made her way into the house and took a good long look at herself in the mirror. She had been working hard to lose weight, to be in better shape. She was down 20 pounds but she still hated the way she looked. Aside from her friends and her little brother, she was alone. In some ways it suited her. She'd had one serious relationship and that left her ready to just put the idea of love and romance behind her for good.

After, she made her way into her room to throw on pajamas and spent the rest of the afternoon cleaning until Charlie got out of school. At 12, he was more than a handful of energy. In a week, he would be gone with friends on vacation, and she would really be alone all summer. He had been living with her a year and a half now, but some days it seemed like only yesterday that he had moved in. She was 22 and ready to tackle the world when she got the call. Her parents and her little brother were in an accident.

Like most people, she didn't think anything could happen to her. She rushed to the hospital, but her parents were both gone, leaving Charlie, with her. It was a rough start, but they were good now. She'd be lying if she said she didn't get lonely sometimes though. He kept her busy, one activity to another. Motherhood at her age was not part of her plan, but she was lucky they had each other. That thought brought her back to Braden. She wondered if he had a family. He seemed like a nice guy.

She never had an opportunity to meet her neighbor. As far as she knew the little lady that came in and out on occasion was the only one who visited that house at all. She sighed, she had rambled on and on about nothing, he must have thought her a complete idiot. Finally, she sat down to calculate how to pull off everything this month.

She was a local teacher, well she was a substitute. She was still in school part-time but she was determined to finish. Most of the time she worked enough days to just barely pay the bills, but having a 12 year old with numerous after school activities put a dent in things. Not to mention the rent on this place was out outrageous. Since her parents were renting as well, their place was too much for her to take on.

They were always like the traveling circus, always moving and changing. Chloe didn't want that for her little brother. She lived that life and he needed stability. She would simply have to cut out some things, but first she would have to find what those things were.

Braden walked into his house, well Gerald's and Abbie's house. They left it for him in the will. No children of their own, they took him in and loved him as if he were theirs. He didn't live here, it didn't feel like he should, and to be honest, he didn't want to take over. He liked being able to walk in and see their things as they left it. It gave him a sense of peace. Deep down, he knew it wasn't healthy, he should sell it, but for now he couldn't let go.

He checked on things here and then headed to the place he lived in the hills. He called ahead the week before so that it could be opened up and aired out. He hadn't been here in months and knowing it would be ready was one of the many luxuries he enjoyed. He had a house manager and a housekeeper, both trustworthy friends, and he compensated them well for the work they did for him.

Once he was there, he made his way inside and he poured himself a drink, leisurely making his way to the large windows overlooking the city. He wanted her. The thought crossed his mind and he smiled. Chloe, there was something about her that struck a nerve, and he wanted to figure it out. He thought at first it had been her coy and shy personality, but he had played that game before and knew that wasn't it.

There was a depth to her, and he wanted to know more. Women were always around, throwing themselves at him and offering him their charms. It came with the business... and the money. It was rare he felt connected to someone who didn't know about either of those things. She felt the connection too, but she simply dismissed it, and he wanted to know why. He suddenly smiled as an idea came to mind. She had no clue who he was or the money he made. Even in her wildest dream, would she ever guess that he was a billionaire. He pulled out his phone and called Mike.

Braden pulled up to Mike's townhouse once more with a renewed spirit. Mike had given him the green light at least for the next few weeks. That would be plenty of time to figure Chloe out. He glanced over at her place before heading inside. Much like his penthouse, the place hadn't been lived in in months. Everything shined and gleamed. "Thank you Mrs. Anderson." He said under his breath.

She was a sweet woman, often quiet and reserved, but she could clean the hell out of this bachelor pad. He decided there was no time like the present to start pursuing his curvy neighbor. He made his way over to her door. It wasn't late, so he gave it a knock. She opened the door in a flurry, and as soon as she saw him, she looked shocked.

"Braden hello." She smiled at him and he felt the heat rising in him. Her hair was pulled up on top of her head and she was wearing a t-shirt and sweats. Casual and damn near the sexiest thing he had ever seen.

"Hello Chloe, thought I'd see if you were up for a chat? It's just that I've been out of town and it's hard to get resettled." He gave her a smile and gauged her reaction.

She was just a little intimidated. She assumed he would move on and let her be, but here he was, in his tight jeans and arms that looked ready to rip out of his shirt. She gulped slightly, what was wrong with her? She usually had more control over herself than this. She gave him a half smile.

"I wish I could. It's just that my little brother is here and is sleeping." There, that should put him off.

"Oh, I see. Maybe we could sit on the deck?" He shoved his hands in his pockets and she mechanically nodded a yes. He smiled at her again and she moved to let him in.

She must be completely out of her mind. What was she doing? She didn't even know him that well and she just let him walk right into her house. He could be a crazy person or something. She sighed.

"I'm not a killer or anything, if that's what you're worried about." They had made it to the sliding door and he leaned in behind her, whispering it in her ear.

She felt the heat of his breath on her ear and shivered. It had been a long time, very long, and she was just sensitive that's all. They moved out to the deck, and as she shut the door and turned towards him, he was directly in front of her.

"Are you married Chloe?" He leaned towards her as he said it, propping his arm against the sliding door beside her head.

"You're very forward aren't you?" "No, I'm not, said Braden, are you?" She ducked through his arm and made her way over to the wrought iron chairs on the deck. It was dark out there. Having forgotten the deck lights were blown, she silently cursed. She turned around again, and this time he walked over to the rail. She joined him there, waiting and suddenly he turned towards her.

"No, I'm not." He put an arm on either side of her and rested against the railing. As he did so he leaned into her breathing in the scent of jasmine.

She was lost in that moment, He was inches away from her and her only thought was that he must be really desperate to be here with her. More than anything else, she didn't want to look like a fool, it's happened before and she didn't want to go through that again. She dipped below his arm and faced the trees again. She could hear his chuckle, and she frowned.

"You are something else Chloe, you know I want to kiss you, but you keep running, why?"

She looked at him, surprised by his admission. "Why do you want to kiss me? I'm sure you have plenty of other women to kiss, besides, I don't even know you, Braden."

"What better way to get to know me, Chloe." He stood and gave her a smile.

There was something about the way he said it that left her wondering if he was serious or simply out of his mind. She shook her head and turned back around.

"Don't be ridiculous Braden."

She said it simply and he realized she meant it. He frowned as he thought about it. Maybe she wasn't attracted to him. There was only one way to find out. He slid over to the right and grasped her hand in his and pulled her towards him. He saw the look of surprise on her face as he put his hand against the back of her head, pulling her into his arms as his mouth crushed hers.

She was on fire and he did nothing but add fuel to it. She felt his mouth nip at her lips and then dive deeper. She opened her mouth to him, unconsciously meeting his kiss eagerly. As their tongues danced, she felt the fire inside begin to build and grow. It had been so long, and he was very good. She felt his hands then start to move. First, slowly he ran them down her back and over the curve of her hip, pulling her even closer to him. She felt his mouth slowly leave her lips and trail down her neck and he nipped her collarbone. He moved his hands up her hips and his mouth found her again. The kiss was passionate and full of promise. She felt his hand slip under her shirt and she panicked, pushing him away.

Braden stood frozen, what the hell was wrong with him. He planned on sweet talking... maybe steal a kiss, but this... He ran his hand through his hair and walked to the deck to calm himself. One thing was for sure. She wanted him just as badly as he wanted her, she couldn't deny that now. He looked over at her, she was stone-faced and looked almost sad. He frowned, that was not what he expected to happen, but why would it make her sad?

"Chloe, I'm sorry." I didn't mean to get so carried away." She looked down and then back up at him, a smile now sitting on her face.

"I understand. Like you said, you haven't been home in months. I'm sure you're just tired." She moved to walk back to the door leading to the house. She whispered to herself "Plus it's dark out here, I'm sure that helps."

"Helps with what?" He was beside her, he was like a cat the way he moved.

"Nothing sorry, just rambling as always. I should get to bed, I have to be at work early." She smiled at him, but he knew something was wrong here.

"Sure, I understand." He turned to go and then spun back to look at her. "I like kissing you, Chloe. I won't lie about it, and in fact, I want much more than that. I wanted you to know I plan on trying to make sure you know that regularly." He walked down the front steps whistling. She stayed there until she heard his door shut. She leaned her back against the door to try and calm her racing heart.

The days went by quickly, they would often pass each other in the front yards or as they came home. Both of them caught up in work. He consistently asked her to come over for dinner, but she always had reason to say no. He never made any other move to kiss her or otherwise, and she relaxed more around him. They spent two different afternoons sitting out front talking about life, where each time she was sure they had an audience at all times. One afternoon she opened up more than she planned.

"So, Charlie?" Braden asked as Charlie was throwing a ball with a friend in the parking lot.

"My parents were killed in an accident, he was with them, but survived. That was almost two years ago now." She watched Charlie playing. "He is a good boy though."

"That has to be hard on you, suddenly having a 12 year old." Braden watched the expressions changing on her face.

"It took some adjusting, for all of us." She took a sip of water from her glass.

"Why aren't you married?" He asked it very matter of factly, but with a deeper tone to his voice. She turned to look at him.

"I almost was once, actually."

He sat up at her admission. So she had loved someone, being close to them. "You know you have to tell me now Chloe?"

"No, I don't Braden." She stood up, brushing off her skirt as she did and headed into her house. He stood and followed.

She noticed him standing in the doorway. "Really Braden, following me into my own home? Even for you that's a bit much." She started folding the towels on the table in the kitchen. He didn't say anything, but methodically started helping. She paused to look at him and he simply grinned at her. She rolled her eyes.

When they were done, he finally spoke. "Why don't you want to talk about it?"

She put her right hand on her hip. "Because it doesn't matter Braden, that's why." As she turned to go he grabbed her forearm and pulled her to him.

"It does matter Chloe, it certainly is part of why you are the way you are."

"What the hell does that mean "the way I am"?" She felt the sting then. She was different. Why did people always feel the need to point it out to her?

"Wait a minute Chloe what do you think I am talking about here?" He took another step closer, never letting go of her arm.

"Let me go Braden." Her eyes glittered dangerously.

"Not until you tell me."

"Fine." She yanked her arm free. "I was engaged, he seemed to accept me." She gave him a glance. "He was always sweet and kind and then when my parents died, he never made it to the funeral. He apologized, and I was stupid enough to believe him. When Charlie moved in, he tried to force me to send him away to a boarding school of some kind.

He said this was not the future he planned and that Charlie was not his problem. So I refused, and he slept with my friend. I caught them in my friend's house. The worst part was, it had been going on for a long time. She was one of those model-thin blondes. I should have known better." She looked over at him finally and he was in shock. He moved towards her again and she stepped back.

"I'm sorry that happened to you Chloe, he was an ass."

"Thanks."

Her voice was clipped and short now. He knew she was reliving it and it was his fault. He looked at her, she was sad and hurting and it had left something scarred in her. He felt that same feeling when he was put in that home. Like no one understood him or cared to. He didn't want that for her, for her to feel that way. He reached out and grabbed her again and pulled her to him. They stayed that way for a long time, just standing close with him pressed against her until Charlie came running in breaking the spell.

"Chloe, look what I found, a frog!" He happily made his way over to her and she shrieked backing up.

Charlie glanced at Braden, rolling his eyes. "Girls." Braden couldn't help but laugh at the scene before him.

"Well, I have to get going, Chloe. I expect to finish this conversation later." He ruffled his hand in Charlie's hair. "You be nice to your sister." He gave him a smile and he headed out. He had a tremendous amount of paperwork to sort through at his place.

The next week went by uneventfully. She would glance at his place when she went to work, subconsciously hoping to see him. He was a good friend of Charlie, and that was all. School would be out in two days. Finally, it was Saturday, and Charlie was leaving. She knew the Bakers were picking him up at 11 and she started helping him to move his things outside as they waited. He was smiling at her and she finally asked him why.

"You are gonna have a whole lot of time to spend with your new boyfriend next door when I am gone, Sis." He started laughing. She swatted at him.

"Charlie, that's not funny. Keep your voice down. He is not my boyfriend, he is our neighbor."

"Okay, so why is he always asking you out?" He looked up at her and started to laugh again.

"I don't know. Maybe he feels sorry for me because my little brother has such a big mouth." She pushed him as she made her way down the stairs.

"No, he likes you Chloe, I like girls at school... that's how he looks at you." He shrugged at her glare and went back to moving things.

"No, he doesn't, guys like him don't like girls... well like me. That's just the way the world is. It's up to younger guys like you to make the world better." She threw a pillow at him and he scrambled to catch it before it hit the ground. Finally, they noticed the Bakers coming up the side street, and after some time, he was loaded and leaving.

She waved at him, feeling a little sad at the prospect of spending so much time alone. Once it had been easy to fill her time, and now, she was like a mom, and without him, she wasn't sure what to do. She turned around and Braden was there watching her. She gave him a wave and headed back to her house.

He watched her go. It was the longest week of his life and all he wanted to do was touch her. Between issues with the races, complaints from other drivers about a leak, and his manager trying to set him up on random surprise dates at dinner time, he just wanted something normal. He wanted her. He heard what she said and it made sense to him now. "Guys like him and girls like her." She had no idea what he wanted, but he was going to tell her. He took long strides to her door and rang the bell. He felt the anticipation curling up. When she opened the door, he practically fell through it.

"Braden hello..." He cut her off, pulling her to him and covering her mouth with his. He bruised her lips with his attack and she felt her defenses slip away. She thought of nothing but him for a week.

They moved together in the living room and she leaned back on the couch as he pushed her down. She felt the length of him against her and it was perfect. His hands were everywhere and as he unbuttoned her shirt he felt her freeze.

"Look at me Chloe. I want you, all of you just as you are. Stop fighting me." She was still frozen and he knew he had to convince her. He pinned both of her arms above her head with his left arm as he moved his right hand over her curves. She was rounded and smooth, and he loved it. She was aware of every nerve ending in her body, as his hands reached around and under each breast, lifting her bra slightly so that the nipples were exposed. He cupped each globe lovingly until he reached the pert nipple that had hardened under his touch. He pulled and tugged on them, creating a deep ache deep down, soon covering each one in succession with his mouth.

Chloe was lost in the sensation. No one had ever taken time with her like this, ever. His hands were lighting her on fire with every movement.

She was all fire, just like he knew she would be. He was almost in pain with the need to rip off her clothes and bury himself inside her, but he wanted to go slow, wanted it to be good for her too. She was laid out on the couch, her hair, a red flaming swirl around her head and yet he could still tell she was nervous. He moved lower to make a final step in making her his.

Her eyes flew open as she felt him slide his hand under her and lift her off the bed as he loved her with his mouth. She couldn't move, couldn't do anything but feel the way he felt against her. She felt the tension fade away and the mounting pleasure begin to spiral out of control. Her legs were shaking as she climbed that ultimate peak to release. She let go of her resolve and fears and put her hands in his hair and let go.

He felt her release, and the way her legs were trembling made him ache for her more. He moved above her and watched her face as he moved to push inside her. She was tight, and it took more than one pushed to fully envelope himself within her. With a final push, he was exactly where he needed to be. He pushed her knees up and over his shoulders as his movements became more frantic, more demanding. Soon, he stood back from her, one hand holding each knee as he pounded into her relentlessly. He heard her moans, and knew she was sharing in the intensity. Her hips moved with his, and the explosion was powerful as he pushed into her one last time and release came.

They both lay there, trying to breathe and trying to make sense of what just happened. For Chloe, it was unlike anything she ever experienced. She looked up at him and he was smiling down at her. He leaned in and kissed her lightly before he stood up. She once again marveled at his chiseled body. He saw her glance and smiled at her. Hopefully she knew that he found her sexy and he enjoyed touching her. He made his way to the kitchen and Chloe quickly redressed. What had she done? She felt the blush rising up her face. He had seen her, all of her. No one ever had. She made her way into the bathroom and then followed him in the kitchen.

His phone rang and she turned to look at him and he frowned as he listened.

"Chloe, I have to go. I'm sorry, something came up."

"Sure it's fine go ahead." She felt the same fear from before, he would leave now.

"Chloe look at me." She did. "I will be back, I promise. " He kissed her quickly on the head and left.

To say he was worried was an understatement. The twenty minute drive took him 12. He pulled into his lot and stared up at the flaming mess. His penthouse was on fire and all he could do was watch. He found the house staff and was happy they were okay. The three of them watched as the fire department did their best.

The next few days Braden spent sifting through what had once been his home. His home hadn't been saved and very little else had either. He had to meet with the investigator today and then the adjuster. The police assumed this was an accident, but he wasn't as sure. He was staying at a nearby hotel, trying to hold it all together, but barely. He made sure the staff had rooms and that they were well taken care of. Most of his time was spent on the phone or on conference to various media networks and the racing team. He thought about Chloe, her smile and her sweetness. He missed her. Everything he put into proving he liked her the way she was vanished the night he left, and hadn't come back. He promised, and now she would never trust him again.

Chloe knew she was a fool. She spent that entire night waiting for him, as if she believed in his story, or that he would come back. She waited, and the joke was on her. Life had, inevitably gone back to normal. As a teacher, she threw herself back into the work of planning for the next school year. She found that by journaling a lot, she was able to keep her heart from hurting too much.

The reality was she cared about Braden and what he thought of her. The times they spent talking was a big part of that. He was a kind and sweet guy, despite his obvious fetish for big girls. It wasn't that he never came back that night. The fact was he had never come back at all, until yesterday. She hadn't actually seen him, just that his lights were on and music was playing inside. How he could just ignore her now was the brunt of the pain.

She wished for a moment that she had the strength to march over there and demand an answer, but it was better off left alone. She glanced at the clock and headed out to go grocery shopping. As she did, she heard the door open next door and she cringed. The last thing she wanted was a run in. She turned around and it was a woman, a very thin, very hot blonde woman. The blonde in question gave her a wave and she straightened her shoulders and left.

Braden had cancelled the rest of the afternoon and made the decision to try. He had to explain, and most importantly, he had to tell her the truth. He drove to her place and waited. He saw her car, he knew she was there, but for the first time since he was a child, he was scared. He was a nationally known bike racer and had been with more than a few women all over the world and this one woman had him questioning everything about himself. He felt the guilt like a punch in the stomach. Not just for leaving her like that, but for not telling her the truth about who he was. He finally got out of the car and went to the door.

She heard the knock and frantically made her way to the door. She found a solution to her financial woes and was moving in a roommate. To say the mess from what had once been storage was everywhere, would be putting it mildly. She climbed over the final boxes and pulled the door open. There he stood.

"What do you want Braden, I am really busy." She hoped the nonchalant way she talked to him would fool him.

"We need to talk Chloe, really talk." He sounded serious and she finally made eye contact. Still gorgeous, he looked rough. He looked tired and she knew something was wrong. She moved out of the way and he came inside.

He felt a sense of panic at the mess. "Are you moving?" He glanced around.

"No, I found a roommate. Nice guy, good job." She crossed her arms in front of her and waited. She would let him speak, but she wouldn't make it easy for him.

Braden felt a rush of anger. He would be damned if some "guy" was moving in here. "There are some things I need to tell you and explain. I need to know you will let me explain it all and then we will talk about this "guy" you think is moving in here."

He made his way to the living room and she followed. Her arms were crossed again and her eyes were flashing fire. Even now, he wanted her.

He turned the channel to ESPN and turned to look at her. "This is the best way I know how to explain."

She sat there stunned watching sports news, which she didn't even know existed. Some bike racer had a house that burned down and, wow, he was local. She suddenly felt sick. He was everywhere, pictures and stories and she knew. He turned it off.

"Oh my God Braden, are you ok?" She looked at him and touched his hand.

"I'm fine, my house is gone though. That's where I have been. That's why I didn't call."

"Why didn't you tell me you were famous? It would have made our fling that much more memorable for me." She gave him a half smile.

"Stop it Chloe, I don't look at you like that and I know you don't either. It's more than that and you damn well know it." She moved off the couch and towards the door. He caught her hand as she went by, standing up in the process. He kissed her forcefully, only letting go when they needed air. It was then he noticed her tears. He kissed her eyelids and wiped them away.

"Don't cry Chloe, please, I'm so sorry for everything." He pulled her into his arms and buried his head in her hair.

He kissed her face and then her mouth again. It started so simply, wanting to comfort each other, and soon they were lost in the moment. She pulled away from him and went up the stairs, and he followed. Once there, he took the lead, grabbing her hand and pulling her with him into the room. Their actions frantic now, they undressed each other. He turned her around to face away from him. She felt him unzip her dress and trail his fingers down her spine as the dress slipped to the floor. He reached around to cup her breasts, which overflowed in his hands. He pulled her back against him and she felt the hardness there.

"Don't ever question what you do to me Chloe, feel what you do."

She did just that, taking him into her hand and feeling the length of him. He pushed her over towards the bed and she climbed into it and he stopped her. She was half on and half off the bed when he moved behind her. He filled her suddenly and quickly, and she gasped at his entry. He moved his hand up to her hair, winding his fist in it and bracing himself as he plunged into her faster, and deeper. They moved together both seeking and searching for something. She was the first to reach her peak and she moaned out his name as she did so pushing him over the edge as well. He pulled her to him spooning behind her. She was his, and she always will be. Suddenly she stood.

"You should go Braden." She pulled her dress over her head and stood. He stood as well and she was once again reminded of how perfect he was.

"Chloe please."

"Braden this.... this was a mistake. You know it as well as I do."

"No, it's not a mistake, how can you even say that after what just happened?"

"We come from different worlds, Braden, you're... famous for God's sake and I am just some..."She trailed off. "You lied to me, Braden."

"I know, at first I just wanted you. I was driven by a need to be inside you, loving you. Then things changed."

"No, they didn't Braden... ...you should go... now."

He saw the firm set of her jaw and knew she was serious. He took one last look at her before he left. Chloe waited until she heard the front door shut and she locked it before crumbling to the floor and gave over to the tears.

Braden was not himself. His driving was awful and he couldn't connect with the course. He normally would love the flowing hills of Virginia, but he was officially not on a streak anymore. He angrily threw his helmet into the seat of the car and made his way to the crew. They all knew to avoid him when he was like this. Braden angry was a rare thing, but it usually had a quick turnaround. This time he was like this all day. He was angry, and worried. Chloe refused to respond to any messages he sent her and he missed her. She was so damn stubborn and it hurt that she didn't feel the same way.

Braden made his way into the hotel and caught a glimpse of himself in the mirror. He was dirty from the race, but he was changed now. He spent his entire adult life alone until this one woman came into it and now he was worried about someone else. He knew she had been struggling, in more ways than one. She shared her situation with him, told him her secrets, and he lied to her. He knew she was hurting, but couldn't she see how he felt? He frowned. How did he feel exactly? He got into the shower to wash away everything from the long day. He had to do something, and soon.

He met up with Mike for dinner that evening who put it all in perspective for him.

"You're in love with that chubby girl back home aren't you?"
Braden stood and towered over him.

"Don't ever say that about her again, do you understand me?"
"Whoa, whoa buddy calm down. I didn't mean anything negative about it. I am just telling you man, you got it bad. The whole damn crew is afraid of you the way you're tearing things up all the time. Not to mention you lost your streak, you need to see her and make it right. Either let her go or marry the girl."

Braden sat back in his chair and thought about what he said. Marry her? The thought gave him a start of panic, but the idea of coming home to her, all the time was one he could love. He ran his hand through his hair. He hoped she and Charile were okay, if only she would answer his damn calls. He suddenly had an idea, one that might make her call him after all. He pitched his idea to Mike, who chuckled and started to make the call.

Chloe was frustrated. The roommate was an ass and he left his things all over her house. More importantly, he was indifferent to Charlie. Treating him like a bug in his way all of the time. Last night was the final straw. He came home drunk and groped her, and she was finished with it. She took a deep breath before knocking on his door. She had to do it repeatedly before he finally yelled something and stumbled to open it.

"What Chloe?" He moaned as she pushed the door open wider.

"You have to move, Josh. I can't have this kind of environment for Charlie."

"You can't just kick me out, Chloe. I have rights. Besides, you like it when I touch you, don't even try to lie." He took a step towards her and grabbed her again. This time she pushed at him and scratched his face. He gave her one blow to the face and she staggered backwards. She rushed to the living room calling for Charlie and the two of them made their way out to her car.

Mrs. Anderson watched the little car pull away with a shake of her head. That was a bad man in there, she saw her holding her face when they left. She pulled out her phone to call Mikey and tell him the plan couldn't work now. After Mike hung up the phone, it took him a minute to turn around. He knew once he told Braden, he would lose it. There was nothing he could do but to tell him.

"Well, what did she say?" Braden was eager to hear Chloe was ok.

"Seems like she is gone man, I mean she had a couple bags and she and Charlie left."

"What the hell do you mean they left?"

"Sit down man I'll tell you everything."

Braden did, only because he knew he wouldn't get any information otherwise.

Twenty minutes later, Braden called the airline and booked a flight to Texas. The sonofabitch was going to pay and he would be the one to do it. Mike tagged along, mainly because he didn't want Braden to end up in jail. They took the direct flight and Braden was full of tension and ready to fight the entire time. Finally on the ground, they picked up a rental car and made their way into the city. He was practically out of the car before it even stopped. He made his way to her house and when the door opened, he let the first punch fly.

Mike glanced down at the man on the floor. The guy didn't even have a chance. Braden knocked him out with two hits. Braden made his way upstairs and checked to make sure she had yet to come back. He wasn't sure where she would go, she had a few friends, but no one she spoke about enough to give him any clear direction to head in. He walked back over to Mike's and sat in the chair by the window so he could watch and wait. He glanced up at Mike.

"Give me your phone."

"Why?"

"Just trust me, I'll give it right back."

He took the phone from Mike and sent a text to her from his number. He visibly relaxed when he got a response. It was wrong, but it had to work. She would be furious, but he would at least get to look at her and make sure she was ok.

Chloe was concerned. The message said that she needed to come home right away. She wasn't even sure who sent her the message, but she had to find out what was going on. She dropped Charlie off at a friend's house and made her way home quickly. She had so much to figure out and she was exhausted. She glanced at herself in the mirror. It had only been a number of hours, but her right eye was purple and bruised.

She couldn't go back in there. He was horrible. What had ever possessed her to let him move in in the first place? Money, always money. She wanted to keep Charlie in one place with his friends, something she never had, and this is what happened. She pulled into her parking lot and got out of the car. She would wait out here. She couldn't go in there alone ever again. It was then that the door next door opened and she saw him.

It was only a couple of months, but he was perfect. He took a few long strides to get to her and before she could say a word, he wrapped himself around her and picked her up. He literally picked her up. She heard him whisper her name and she closed her eyes against the emotional overflow she felt inside her. Why was he here? She pulled away and he stood back looking her over. When he looked at her face, he swore.

"That asshole." He started walking towards her place and she went after him.

"Braden wait." She went behind him and they made it to the door. She grabbed his arm. Suddenly there was another man there. He pulled Braden away.

"Calm down man." Braden turned towards her as the police pulled up out front.

"Oh no, Braden the police?" She walked towards the car again. She felt his hand on her arm.

"Yes, the police Chloe. Look at your face and what he did to you." She tentatively touched her face with her fingertips. She saw the rage fill his face again and she touched him. "I'm fine Braden, really."

He watched her go speak to the police and he glanced at the front door as it slowly opened. Josh came staggering out and Mike once again grabbed Braden by the arm, preventing him from going to jail. The police made their way over to Josh and cuffed him. After they were gone, Braden turned to face her.

"We need to talk Chloe, now." He went inside and she soon followed, but not before Chloe saw the blond from before walking hand in hand with Mike. So she was never with Braden. Somehow that helped to make her feel a little better. At a wave from the two of them, she made her way inside where Braden was waiting.

"Braden, nothing has changed. I love that you came here to help me, I do, but we are still so different. Everything we do is..." She stopped as he kissed her. She closed her eyes, even if they couldn't be together, she could enjoy the way it felt when he kissed her, even just for another moment. She relaxed in his arms and he felt it. He pulled her even closer to him and ran his hands over her curves.

She was everything, and he wanted all of her. The kiss intensified and he undid the back of her dress pulling it to the floor. She was lost in him, his touch and felt the coolness of the air against her skin. She trusted him unlike she had ever trusted anyone else. He pulled her into the living room never stopping the kisses he trailed down her neck. When they made it there, she stopped him. She could be herself with him, for the moment. She walked around him and shed the rest of her clothes. She walked to the couch and laid back on it, fully unclothed and waiting. He watched her, his mouth hungry to touch her, but reveling in the way she was with him now.

She was no longer concerned about if he was attracted to her, or if he wanted her. She believed in him and how much he wanted to touch her. He finally moved towards her, gently moving his mouth down her chest, stopping to kiss and run his tongue over each crested peak. He buried his face in her breasts pulling on them and kissing every inch of them. She had her hands in his hair now pulling his head back up to kiss her deeply. He moved his hands along her curves and she arched up to meet them.

She moaned at the sensation and was aching for him with a need deep down. This is how he wanted her, how he needed her to be with him. He moved his fingers over her, working to a fevered state and he watched the expression on her face as she became more demanding of release. He wanted to give her more and he slid down, burying his face in her and tasting her.

He felt her hands in his hair as she grinded into him and finally he felt her reach that ultimate peak and he knew it was time. He raised above her, his excitement evident and she stood to touch him. Sliding her hands down his body over his chest and further until with a swift intake of breath, she held him in her hands. She slid to the floor, and when he saw her look up at him, it was almost too much. He pulled her up to him and kissed her deeply before pushing her to the couch again.

He mounted her swiftly, pushing into her depths. He reached the full hilt of himself and stopped. He wanted to just feel her surrounding him like this. He looked up at her face. She was flushed from her climax and eager for more, but he wanted to watch the expressions as he moved her. He moved slowly now stretching her to her limits and testing himself, his ability to prolong the inevitable.

He felt her hands on his chest as he looked down at her and he watched her curvy body move with his. He wanted her, always. He pulled out and slammed back into with a force that shook them both to the core. It had never been this good, this satisfying. The need was far too great and they both were aching to reach that final release. He moved faster now, steadily grinding into her and she was almost whimpering, and calling for him. He loved her like this, with abandon.

He increased his speed and was both grinding and pounding into her at the same time. It was good, too good. She called his name as her body moved on its own. She was no longer in charge of it and she felt the orgasm start low until it shuddered through her entire body, leaving her spent and breathless. Her explosion rocked him to the core and he couldn't hold back any longer. He slid his hands under her and lifted her off the bed slightly as he plunged into her again and again until he shared in her release. He buried himself inside her as far as he could. He wanted her to know he had given it all to her.

They lay there holding on to each other. Both afraid to speak, afraid to break the beauty of what they had shared. He knew she would run from him now, but he wouldn't let her. He was in love with her and he couldn't imagine life without her in it. She was the first to move, raising her head to look at him.

"Braden." She whispered and he gently kissed her lips. He held her that way, the two looking at each other waiting for the other to say something else. She was what he had been missing his entire life, she was family.

She raised up, suddenly self-conscious of her nakedness. He knew the person she was in the throes of passion was not who she was every day. It was a part of her she shared with only him, and he loved her all the more for it. He pulled her dress from the floor and helped her into it. He noticed she relaxed some and glanced at him sheepishly as she did it.

"Chloe, before you say anything, I need you to know something." He moved the strands of hair that had fallen into her face as she moved. She waited and looked up at him.

"I am in love with you." I know you don't know how this will work, but I know you have feelings for me too. I know you worry about everything, from yourself, to Charlie and money, and this house."

"Braden" she started, but he held up a hand to her...

"I'm not finished. The last few months have been the worst kind of hell for me. I found my mother dead on my living room floor when I was twelve, and aside from a loving couple who gave me a family for three years, I have been alone my whole life. I didn't even know what I was missing until you and Charlie. I love you. Chloe. I want you with me... you and Charlie. I have more money than I can ever spend and I want to share everything with you."

"Braden... I love you too." He relaxed with her words and pulled her closer to him. She was worried about life with Braden, what she never considered was how awful life would be without him. She smiled up at him and asked.

"Will you miss all the models and thin girls? Can I really satisfy you, Braden?

"Chloe, what we have is better than anything I have ever done in my whole life. You are sexy and gorgeous, and ALL I want is you." She smiled and a giggle escaped.

"What's so funny?"

"Charlie said you liked me even before any of this. Now I have to tell him he was right."

"I love you Chloe."

He kissed her again, and for the first time in her life, she believed it.

****

The Billionaire's Desire

Alexander Jacobs knew his life would be different from now on. Nothing could prepare him for the changes coming. Had he known, he would have done something differently, prepared somehow. He would have tried to make his father proud of him, and he would have loved his mother more.

He hung his head in his hands. There was nothing he could do now. His life was changed, and all he had left to focus on was tomorrow. His life was quiet now, too quiet.

His parents were both gone. They were killed by a drunk driver, he had no siblings, and only a few friends he could count on one hand, friends he could trust that is.

He sat back in the high backed chair and took a deep breath. Even the friends he did have were busy with their own lives. He was 23, still too young to know what he was doing most of the time, and now he was going to have to run a business that he hadn't much thought about before.

He enjoyed the fruits of the family business. He always had everything he needed or wanted. He was spoiled and selfish. He shook his head. Now he had to grow up.

Alex glanced up at the clock on the mantle. The meeting started at 2. That gave him ten minutes to get his head together. He started rifling through the ledger on his desk, trying to prepare for the day ahead.

His parents had been gone almost a week. The funeral was yesterday. They deserved more...deserved better. He would do his best to make them proud. He knew he would have to because there was no one else who could.

The only bright spot in his life yesterday at the funeral was Brienne. Brienne Warhol had been there. He remembered the day he first saw her in 4th grade. She was all elbows and freckles with her long red hair in braids. She was beautiful. They grew up on the same street, or close to it.

She was always a gangly tomboy, playing in the dirt and riding bikes with the boys while all the other girls were happy playing inside with Barbie and practicing with makeup and nail polish. He smiled thinking about the 6th grade dance.

He prepared to ask Brienne for weeks, but she never seemed to notice he was there. She was always busy with everything else. Most of the boys thought of her as one of them, but not Alex. He was very much aware of the fact that Brienne was a girl. He had it all planned out and walked up to her at lunchtime. She was sitting at a table with some of their friends all arm wrestling each other. He took a deep breath and simply said:

"Brienne, will you go to the dance with me?" He said it casually despite his racing heart and had taken his usual seat across from her while waiting on a response.

"Sure." She said it so quickly he had to look at her to catch her eye and make sure she was actually responding to him. She gave him a slight smile and set out to arm wrestle, and beat, Bobby Anderson on the next match.

His dad sent him in the company car to pick her up the night of the dance and he was terrified. She came down the stairs in a green dress and her hair all brushed out. It looked just like fluffy orange cotton. She was beautiful. He opened the door for her, and once they were inside, she started chattering away about school and how these girl shoes were so dumb.

He just let her talk. He liked the way she went on and on. He was always the quiet one and she didn't know how to be. It may have been because she had no mother, and her dad was doing the best he could with her. Whatever the reason, she always had a lot to say.

They pulled into the school parking lot and immediately their group of friends gathered around. It was just like any other school day.

At some point she had braided her hair so it would stop "flying all over the place" as she put it. The rest of the night was spent with the group of friends. No dancing, and certainly not what he planned.

He shook his head and smiled as he was brought back to the present. She came to the funeral. She was there for him, and he loved her all the more for it. They were friends now, not as close, but still friendly enough.

She would send him emails from school and he would write back talking about whatever was going on in their sleepy town of Dale City Virginia, as well as what was happening to their friends and who was moving and who had come back.

He enjoyed the way she would write about her classes, which ones were easy, and which were harder for her, and the way men seemed to always want to ask her out and not ask her opinions. She had gone off to New York after high school. She always dreamed of going there, and since her goal was Columbia Law, she thought her best option was doing her undergraduate work there as well.

Brienne always worked hard to do well. Alex would frequently ask her if she needed anything and she always told him no. She was defiant and determined to succeed. He admired that in her. He went to college locally at Mary Washington and studied Business. He didn't have a clue what he wanted to do and his father told him it was a great back up for whenever he figured it out.

Today he was thankful for that. Seeing Brienne yesterday after such a long time felt good. Gone were the braids and freckles, and in their place, was a sophisticated woman. She was still as beautiful as the day he met her. He never even had a chance to speak with her though. She gave him a wave at one point, and he smiled back.

She was rarely in town, and when she was, he always tried to make time for her. They would usually eat Chinese take-out and laugh and listen to music from the year they graduated. The last time she visited was over two years ago. Even then, she hadn't strayed much from The

Brienne of middle school. It was obvious something changed. Yesterday, he was surrounded by his parents' friends and business associates. By the time he was able to get a few moments alone, she disappeared.

It would be easy to find her. Still in the same house, her father lived down the street. They lived in the cul-de-sac of the neighborhood off the loop that led to his house.

Alex's parents were wealthy and enjoyed living in a mansion. They planned to have more children but it never come to pass. Brienne's house was part of the mill town and he knew he would find her there.

He had every intention of going to see her tonight. After this meeting of course. He stood and grabbed his paperwork, took a deep breath and headed down the corridor. He could do this.

Two hours later, Alex pulled forcefully on the tie at his throat. What a mess. The merger was two days away when his parents were killed. He wanted to go home and grieve but this paperwork had to be done before something, or someone, showed up to rock the proverbial boat.

He spent two hours being briefed about acquisitions and merger paperwork. The logistics of operations and the appointing of officers to manage the foreign accounts was making his head spin, but he had to learn every detail of the business.

The only person he trusted was Jameson, who was his father's trusted advisor and best friend. He was the one who prepped him for today and the one who would help him take the business to the next level. Alex would be fine, he had no other choice.

Alex headed home to organize the pieces of his life he could still control and to change and relax before tackling the next big thing that would inevitably come up. The driver pulled up to the gate and they moved on until they rounded the front of the house.

Not really one for the rules, Alex jumped out of the car as they stopped. He refused to wait for the chauffeur to open the door for him. He was capable and refused to follow all of the rules.

He bounced up the front stairs and opened the door to the main hall. He could smell his mother's perfume when he entered the house. He hoped it would always be that way, but sadly time erases everything. He made his way upstairs and changed into jeans and a t-shirt.

He was sure being seen in town like this was something frowned upon now that he was the head of the business. He was suddenly forced to become his father. The thought made him cringe as his father had been stern and fair, but not easily approachable. His mother was the nurturer and his father the businessman.

Alex ran a hand through his black hair and looked at his reflection for a moment. He had lines around his eyes. The stress was already taking a toll and it had been days. He had short black hair and blue eyes. Not unattractive he supposed.

He dated his fair share of women and enjoyed having fun and meeting new people. He would figure out his new life as he went. He shrugged and grabbed his jacket as he headed out. He decided to walk. The April air was crisp and clean, and it helped him to clear his head.

Brienne always had something to say that would make sense, make it better. She never indicated she was interested in Alex at all. Once upon a time he thought she was the one for him, but instead, become good friends. That was worth so much more than romance or sex. He walked the ¼ mile in silence thinking about his parents. They loved each other very much. They were always together and the night of the accident had been no different.

His father had been hosting a dinner to raise funds for one of his business mergers. His mother accompanied with him, ever devoted to her husband. They said goodbye to Alex that night as he watched television in the den eating a snack. He yelled a hello and gave them a wave and a glance before they left. Why didn't he go say goodbye the right way, why hadn't he hugged his mother? The fact that he barely gave them a wave made his resolve that much stronger. He would make his parents proud.

He made his way up the drive of the house Brienne grew up in. It was small and quaint but clean. Even now, her ten speed bike was propped up against the side of the house. Untouched in years, it was a symbol of a childhood long gone. She opened the door before he even knocked.

"Alex." She smiled at him and opened the screen door and came out on the porch. She hugged him tightly. "I'm so sorry about your parents." She stood back and he took her in. She was more beautiful than he could remember. She finally tamed her hair and was dressed in a black dress. She was elegant and he was lost.

"My dad is getting his treatments so I thought I should come outside to you." She walked over to the swing on the porch. Her father was sick, he thought. She had such a hard life growing up but she was strong. They sat on the swing together for a few moments and chatted about the weather. She asked about work and he shared and she told him about school and how soon after she graduated she would be going to Columbia. She had been accepted.

"Hey brat you made it in?" He sat up quickly.

"Yes I did." She nearly sparkled with the excitement.

"Wow that's great Brie. You worked so hard and I know you're excited." He grabbed her hand and gave her a squeeze.

"Thanks, I am overwhelmed really. I have so much to do to get ready and...well there is a lot." She smiled at him.

"Well we have to go to dinner tonight and celebrate, my treat." He offered and she accepted.

"We never get to hang out anymore, like old times." She sighed. "It was so much easier when we were kids. No one was sick and we all had each other. We had our family and friends." She sighed.

"It certainly has changed, you're still a brat though." He looked at the tree across the street, thinking. He stood up to go. "I'll pick you up at 6, and wear something nice." He smiled at her as she stuck her tongue out at him. He made his way back up the hill towards the bend in the road which would lead back to his house.

Damn you Alex. She watched him leave. He was so handsome, and that was all she could think about. It made it hard for her to concentrate when he looked at her. She hated the way he called her brat. He'd done it since they were in middle school. She looked down at the slippers she was wearing.

They were so different, she and Alex. Once upon a time she thought he had a crush on her. It was probably at that horrible dance in 6th grade when she figured out he just wanted to be friends. He picked her up and she tried so hard to look pretty.

Her father enlisted help from the neighbor to help with "girl stuff." They did their best. No one knew about conditioner yet and her hair was always so unruly. He picked her up and they went to the dance. She talked him to death. It's what she did when she was nervous.

Everyone thought she was just one of the guys and in some ways, she was. She loved playing football and wrestling and she hated getting dressed up. But there was something about Alex that made her feel funny. Looking back she knew it was because he made her feel like a girl. Feeling like a girl was a new idea for her that was for sure. Once they arrived at the dance mean Mary Jenkins pulled her aside in the bathroom and told her about the "bet".

The boys all bet that she would be "different" if she dressed like a girl. So she knew then they were testing her, fearful their friendship would be gone for good. So she braided her hair in the bathroom and went back to being one of the guys. She refused to allow her heart to hurt because she wanted Alex to like her. They were all friends and that was more important than anything else and they didn't want to lose her.

Even now she shook her head as she thought about it. The entire "group" was disbanded by now. Two of the group members left for the military. One was a teacher in town, one was killed in a boating accident, one was a police officer two towns over, and then there was she and Alex. It was funny that they were the only two who didn't have people in their lives. That alone made no sense. Alex was not only the most eligible bachelor in Dale City, he was gorgeous to boot. It made no sense at all.

She picked the pillow cushion on the seat as she swung lightly. She was no angel. She dated her fair share of men. Most of them where playboys and only wanting one thing from her. As she took her education more seriously, they took her less seriously. What she wanted was an equal, but who knew if that even existed. Alex was always out of her league anyway, he was rich, refined and charming, and she was all tomboy and barely had enough money to get through school.

Even today he in his designer jeans and she in her slippers with a hole in the big toe. She laughed lightly. They were on opposite ends of reality but they were friends and that was enough for her. She sighed, time to check on her father.

She made her way through the house and cringed. It was a mess. She hated leaving him alone for so long. She hadn't been home in two years. It was just too expensive to come home, she needed every penny for school. He said he understood but it was hard for him. He had gotten sick some time ago and it never seemed to go away.

He had breathing treatments and on the phone he always told her he was fine, being here now she knew he had been lying. The house was turned upside down. TV dinners and coffee seemed to be a staple for him and he had no one to come check on him. She found a clean spot on the couch in the living room and sat down to start planning her course of action and what she would tackle first.

A few hours later she looked around her. It was better than she had expected. She scrubbed every inch of the living room and kitchen.

There wasn't a speck of dirt on anything and the four large trash bags on the front porch was a testament to her hard work. She was filthy. Her hair in braids and wearing jeans and a tank top, she was a visible mess.

Her father spent the afternoon resting and it wasn't until there was a knock on the front door that she even considered how long she had been at it.

She opened the front door to find Alex standing there. He was perfect. Blue suit and tie white shirt. His hair brushed back, he could have been on the cover of a magazine. She stood there for a moment before the realization set in that she had been working much longer than she realized. He smiled at her and it brought her back to reality quickly.

"Alex, I ...well see the thing is." She looked down at herself and he cut her off.

"I'm early brat, you have time to get ready unless you want to change the plan and do something more industrial?" She threw a rag at him and he chuckled. The truth was she was adorable. Hair in braids and cleaning, it was like he stepped back in time for a moment. He needed that moment. He felt normal even if for only a few moments. He settled onto a bar stool and watched her head upstairs to get ready.

"I'll hurry Alex, I promise." She called down the stairs to him.

"Just wash your hair, whatever you do, I think I saw a candy bar wrapper in there." He smiled.

He heard the bathroom door shut and the water come on. She always kept him amused if nothing else. He looked around the house. Her father was alone here and it was cozy. He much preferred a smaller space when being alone. It was nice - almost like the house was hugging you. Unlike the space Alex had at home. He was alone in a tremendous amount of space.

She bounded down the stairs and the transformation was astounding. She straightened her hair somehow and was wearing a dark blue dress with a square cut neckline and black pumps. Her face was alive with pink cheeks and some light gloss on her lips. Otherwise she was without make up.

"You gonna stare at me like I have two heads or are we going, Mr. Jacobs?" She put her hands on her hips and tapped her foot. He shook himself free of his thoughts and stood so they could go. The drive was pleasant and uneventful. He decided to drive them himself and made reservations in the town nearby.

They had reservations for 7, and he knew she was always multitasking so his early arrival was on purpose. They dined on oysters and salads, and he ordered steak for his main course. She had the fish. They chatted about the past and who was where. It was over dessert when a burly looking man came over to say hello.

"Alex and Brie...now if Junior and Jerry were here I'd be rich right now." He smiled and Alex stood and embraced his friend. Brie did the same and kissed Brandon on the cheek. He was part of the "group" and had managed to stay close by. He wasn't in uniform but Alex knew he become a cop a year or so ago. He was always the jokester of the group which made his profession that most interesting. He had always been the one to get them into trouble and now he was the one enforcing the rules.

"Just look at you two, how long has it been two three years?" Alex motioned for him to sit and he did so.

"My buddies and I are out celebrating a big bust we took down earlier today. I have to get back but after seeing "Red," over here." He hooked his thumb towards Brie. "I just had to come say hello."

Brie smiled at him. "You look great and congrats on the bust."

"I look the same, you on the other hand look great." He leaned towards her obviously flirting and joking at the same time.

"Sorry to hear about your folks Alex man, really. I was at the funeral but you were surrounded by people." He sobered for a moment.

"Thanks Bran that means a lot to me." Alex took a long drink. "So why would you be rich?"

"Oh yea that." He chuckled "A long time ago Jerry and Junior and I made a bet on who was going to marry Brie. They said Mason but not me, I said Alex. We all put two bucks in and buried it under the old cotton mill steps." He laughed and they joined in.

"Well we're not married so you'd still not be rich, besides that money was spent a long time ago." Alex smiled at the shocked look on his face.

"Well you two look married enough all fancy and laughing I just assumed..." he trailed off as Brie took a long drink of water. "Wait what do you mean that money was spent a long time ago?"

"Well the thing is Mason and I heard about your bet and we dug that money up and bought soda pop and chips one afternoon. We sat by the old mill and laughed at how we pulled one over on you all." Alex laughed at the look on his face.

"Well damn, and here I thought I had $6 in savings I could count on." He smiled at them and stood up. "I have to get going, y'all look real nice together so don't fight the love people." He sauntered off giving Brie a wink as he went.

"Well Bran has certainly not changed a bit." Brie changed the subject as to avoid and discussion about love.

"Have I told you you look beautiful tonight Brie? I'm slow so I doubt I have but I wanted you to know it."

He gave her a half smile and she blushed. What was wrong with him anyway, he was being awfully flirty. They wrapped up dinner and he headed back to her house. She had always been easy to talk to and having this time together was wonderful. She helped him feel more like himself than he had in a long time. They sat on the porch swing for a while. He wanted to enjoy laughing for a little while longer.

"When do you head back?" He glanced over at her on the swing.

"Tomorrow." She looked down at her hands. "I have registration Monday and classes start next week. I feel like I should turn it all down though. Dad, he is just not well and I worry about him."

"You can't turn it down Brie, you have to go. I can check in on him from time to time. You have worked too hard to quit now."

She looked over at him. "Really, you'll check on him? That's an awful lot to ask of you Alex, you have a company to run." She leaned back.

"Yes really, it will bring me back to reality from time to time." He smiled. He stood up from the swing. He knew if he stayed too long he'd make a fool of himself like he did long ago. She didn't think of him like "that" and he didn't want her to feel uncomfortable. He especially didn't want to ruin their friendship.

He gave her a hug and she leaned into it. If only he didn't think of her like a boy. She knew he didn't want to ruin their friendship, but it was hard not to want him to see who she was now. He was her best friend and that would have to be enough.

"I'll be back in June maybe we can do this again?" She smiled at him.

"Of course you know that." He was being polite in his words when what he wanted to do was kiss her.

They parted ways both thinking of the other. The night was long for them both. What they didn't realize is that life was about to change and it would be much longer than just June before they would see each other again.

Days turned into weeks and then months. Soon it had been a year since his parents had died. Alex was learning his new role proficiently. He had a hand in the last two accounts and things were looking up. He tried to do well and think like his father. It paid off.

He would get an email from Brie from time to time about classes and work but time between them grew wider and wider, she worked all the time it seemed. He checked in on Mr. Warhol every Sunday and he was doing remarkably well. He even had a lady friend that came around. He would leave voicemails for Brie occasionally and tell her about her father, but never heard back.

The months grew longer and the contact slowly grew more sporadic. He was busy with work and it consumed him. He dated a cute blonde from legal for a while a few months ago, but the drive to do better created some distance between the two of them.

He was alone. Once the solitude had frightened him but now he felt solace in numbers and accounting. One day he was reading the papers when he saw an article about a drug bust in Manassas. There on the page was Bran's ugly mug smiling happily like he hadn't a care in the world. He was promoted and Alex smiled. He deserved it. He read the article and was even more surprised that he was getting married as well.

"Well, well, well, Brandon. I can't believe you're taking the plunge." Alex grinned thinking about when he saw him last at the restaurant. He and Brie were having dinner. What was that a year ago now? He shook his head time was flowing by so fast. Brie...he hadn't thought about her in a while. He hoped she was doing well at school. Her curriculum was difficult, that much he knew. He decided to send her a quick email. He hadn't heard from her in 3 or 4 months now.

"Just checking in to say hello, hope your well. Your dad looks great and is happy with his new lady friend. Keep in touch...A

He signed it with his initial as always. He went back to the proposition on his desk, there was always work to be done and this particular company had a lot of excess baggage that would have to be trimmed. He worked through lunch and finally raised his head after the sun went down. Dinner was a rush of snacks and coffee. He rarely had time for anything else.

"Alex, you need to take better care of yourself." Jameson had come into the office and was sitting on the edge of the couch.

"I know Jameson...so you tell me every other day." He said it quietly but with a smile on his face.

"I mean it Alex you need to get out and live, meet a nice girl ..." he trailed off.

"There is no time for all of that, Jameson and you well know it. So much time was lost in the early days when I was learning and now I have to make it right. When I do, I'll go out and have fun as you put it."

Jameson gave a huff as he stood to go. "Lady Alice is here to see you Alex perhaps she can keep you...ah...company for a while." He left and Alex scowled slightly as she came in. She was petite and blonde and liked to be serious. It may have been her education but she rarely laughed as it would make people think she was "a silly blonde" and not take her seriously.

"Hello Alex." She held up her had to stop him from saying anything. "I know we haven't seen each other in a while, but I was hoping we could go over a case I'm working on and at least share a meal. It's a lonely business and I don't have many people I trust. Besides you make me feel smart and pretty, I like that combination and quite frankly, I need some stress relief." She smiled at him.

He was never one for settling down but she was right. It was a lonely existence when you're in this world. She was smart and she was pretty. He could use the distraction. Besides, she presented it as if their relationship could be some kind of business arrangement and, much like her career she was very determined to do things perfectly, their sex life had been no different. He smiled at her.

"Agreed Alice, agreed. I would love to work on it with you, I just can't give you more than you're asking for right this moment." He looked at her directly. He wanted to be honest up front.

"Once I thought I wanted marriage and family Alex, but I can see clearly now that work is a better path for me. I'm happy with friends, with some benefits. I'd rather have someone in my bed I trust than someone I love." She took off her gloves and settled into the sofa as Jameson came back in.

"Dinner?" He glanced towards Alex.

"Yes Jameson, can you order food for us and have one of the drivers pick it up. Miss Alice and I have some work we need to do." He never looked away from Alice, and Jameson smiled. At least this was a start. Time went on for a while and the mutual benefits to the relationship kept both Alex and Alice happy.

She was thriving at work and was looking for new work in a bigger firm. Alex couldn't have been happier at work. Things were thriving and he was content. Each night he went to bed alone which was when he would over think things and what he wanted. He was happy, he had money, and he had a beautiful lover. What was missing? He would go to bed each night wondering why he couldn't just be content. Even Mr. Warhol married his lady friend. Was there more out there?

Brienne was in very much the same position. She worked and worked and never had a moment's peace. The tuition depleted her savings and there was no hope for paying for her final two years unless she worked. She was working in the law library in the mornings, she had classes in the afternoon and evening, and was working in a bar after class at night.

Days seemed to fly by and with her strange hours, time was a relative thing. She needed to go see her father...or at least call him. He met someone and had a quick wedding. She was happy for him, after so long he deserved to be happy. Plus, she knew he was being taken care of. She received an email from Alex a few months ago.

She hadn't even found time to reply to that. She heard he was dating Alice Pope, it was a name that popped up in news articles she read about him. His business was doing well, extremely well from what she understood. She didn't want to bother him with stupid emails from an old friend. He was nice enough to send her a hello and for that she was thankful. She received an invitation to Brandon's wedding but she knew she couldn't make it.

If she missed one day it would only set her back even more. She met a nice guy at work but she had no time to date. His name was Blake and he would often come sit at the bar with her and walk her to her car. They made small talk and he was nice enough.

She knew he wanted more but was concerned about things progressing in a direction that was ultimately going to go badly. Tonight was no exception. He was sitting across the bar laughing with some guy about how the Cowboys were going to beat the Redskins on Monday night. He caught her eye and gave her a wink. He never missed a beat of the conversation and defended his

"Cowboy" honor to a fault. He really was nice. That night after the bar closed, he walked her out and this time he seemed different. He hugged her goodbye and when she turned to go, he pulled her in close for a kiss. She let it go on for a moment, it had been a long time since anyone kissed her. Before she knew it, one thing led to another and she found herself waking up the next day with him in her bed. She stood there now, towel wrapped around her watching him sleeping. It was a fun night, but the connection she was looking for wasn't there. She actually felt bad for letting things get out of hand. She tiptoed into the shower to get ready for the day, not wanting to wake him up and face where things stood now. She ate a quick breakfast, left a note for Blake and headed downtown to Kirby and Bates where she was working. They were prepping for a huge case and it was all hands on deck for sure. She sat in the conference room combing through files and let her mind drift for a second. She felt different somehow, yes she had a fun night but it was something else. Perhaps she just felt old. She smiled.

Alex would tell her she wasn't old, she just lived like it. Alex, he was so different from anyone else. Blake was not Alex....why she even thought it was bothersome enough. She spun around and got back to work. This stack of paperwork would not sort itself, that much was sure. She worked through her day excited about the fact that tomorrow was Saturday. The law firm was closed and she had no classes so she had the day free until work tomorrow night.

This was her day to run all of her errands and get all of her work done. She could also sleep in past 6:30 am. Her only indulgence was ice cream. Every Saturday afternoon she would get comfortable and eat ice cream and watch an old movie. Only one, she had to study and time was precious.

The day dragged on and after her classes she headed home for a quick bite and to get ready for work. At some point Blake left, and even the bed was made. She changed into her other clothes and headed out. Fridays were always crazy, there were people drinking and laughing, and most of the time there was a fight or two over some woman.

Blake wasn't there, which was odd, but he probably had things to do. Finally, as time went on, Brienne found herself looking at the clock more and more. One more hour, and she had almost a free day to herself. She wrapped things up and headed home. She was exhausted.

She was lucky only one year to go and she could take the bar exam and be done. She was 26 and still young enough where she could build a career and eventually be able to relax. She didn't want to be poor and struggle like she had done all of her childhood.

Her father did his best, but it was easier and cheaper to let her just dress and behave like a boy. She was fine with it, as it gave her friends. Besides, she had no idea what she was "supposed" to act like. Her father was her only role model. He worked long hours and she had to fend for herself a lot of the time.

They scraped by enough to keep the house, but food was rare, She went to bed hungry on more than one occasion and she decided she would never do that again. Her career was her foundation and it would make it so that she never went hungry again. She pulled into her lot and made her way to her apartment. It was a small efficiency on the campus. She did tutoring part time three times a week to allow herself the luxury of living alone.

She considered calling Blake but let the idea go. It was fun, but she didn't have time for all of the drama that comes with having a man in her life. Saturday came bright and sunny. She rolled over at it was 8:10. Even that simple thing...sleeping in made her happy. She started her day doing some shopping and settled in at noon for movie time. She frowned because nothing good was on television.

She sighed and turned it off all together and pulled her laptop into her lap. Maybe she could respond to some emails and some articles for her class. Not fun, but it was better than watching TV.

She opened her new emails. She really needed a system. She spent the next two hours replying and writing to professors and classmates, and her father until she finally cleaned the entire thing out. The next email in the list was the one from Alex now 6 months old. Should she? She shrugged.

A,

Life is busy, 1 hear business is doing well, I saw your article in the Times. She is pretty. I hope you're happy.

Yours,

B

She sat back and ate her ice cream, then gave her father a call to listen to all that was happening back home.

Life went on and on. Alex was now in charge of a corporation ranking number three on the stock exchange. He was secure and enjoying life as much as he could. Tomorrow his parents would have been gone three years. Three years ago he sat in the very chair he was in now.

He ran his hand over the cool leather. He not only carried on the business, he also become everything his father wanted him to be and he did it by working hard. Alice moved on and found a position with a firm in Washington. He was alone again. He let his mind drift to thoughts of Brie. She wrote him back and told him Alice was pretty. Why would she say that? Why did he focus on that? He shook his head. Nothing made sense as far as Brienne Warhol was concerned. She found a new life, one that didn't include him. He hadn't seen her in years and only heard from her from time to time.

He sorted through the stack of mail on his desk. He wasn't as overwhelmed now. Experience taught him to know the size of the correspondence and what was probably inside. He found a green postcard and pulled it from the stack. It was an invitation to a graduation. Probably some staff member or associate.

He turned it over and felt his heart race a little faster. It was for Brienne. She did it. She was graduating from Columbia and with honors, no less. He leaned back in his chair and smiled. She hadn't completely forgotten him, he thought to himself. May 15th. He had a little less than two weeks. He called Linda the secretary.

"Yes, Mr. Jacobs?"

"Linda clear my schedule for the weekend of May 14th. I'll be out of town for a few days."

"Yes, Mr. Jacobs. I'll take care of it."

"Thanks Linda, and plan the weekend off for you too, paid of course, you deserve it."

"Thank You, Mr. Jacobs!"

He hung up, thinking about the weekend he would be gone. He hadn't been this excited about something in a long time. He decided to stroll down to Mr. Warhol's and see what his plan was for graduation. He remembered the way he felt when he came down here to check on him.

He always felt like he was helping Brie somehow. She was far enough away to make it hard to see her father and she never had time to come home anymore. Now he was doing well and he felt like he wasn't needed anymore. He knocked on the door lightly and was greeted by a plump older woman who wore a huge smile.

"Alex, come on in...it's been so long. How have you been?" She enveloped him in a warm hug and shut the door behind him.

He blushed slightly. There was something overwhelmingly motherly about her. She was nothing like his mother in looks or stature but she carried the same warm love about her. Mr. Warhol walked into the room and smiled at Alex.

"Alex, we were just talking about you. Brienne called me a couple of weeks ago and asked about graduation and asked about you." He gave Alex a knowing look.

He swallowed hard. She asked about him? "How is she? I never hear from her, but I just assumed she had a lot of classes this final year."

"She is better than good, she is happy to quit one of her jobs and be able to focus on the bar exam for a while. After graduation I think I have her talked into coming home for a few months until she takes the exam. She needs the break because she works so hard." He sighed.

"What has she been doing exactly? I know she had a full course load and was tutoring, but that's all she really told me." He smiled up as Mrs. Warhol handed him a glass of iced tea.

"She never told you about...work?" Mr. Warhol cleared his throat. "I think maybe she was embarrassed about it or just too busy. I wish I was able to help her more. She deserved more from me." He turned somber.

"Mr. Warhol, do you remember when all the neighborhood kids would be playing softball in the field and how we broke Old Mr. Sampson's window?" He smiled remembering.

"Oh yes he was fit to be tied, ole Sampson." Mr. Warhol smiled.

"Do you remember when prom came and the car broke down and we were all stuck over the state line trying to buy beer?" Mr. Warhol busted into a fit of laughter at that one.

"You boys would have been in so much trouble." He grinned at Alex.

"Who saved us? Who paid for ole Sampson's window, who came and got us all and helped fix that car and get it home?" He looked at Mr. Warhol. "That is two of many examples I can give you, but you saved us all. We never even thought to go to any other parent because you were the "cool" parent. We are all thankful for you so don't ever think you didn't give us all something." He smiled over at Mr. Warhol who looked about to cry.

"Thanks for that son, I loved every one of you. You protected Brie, kept her from getting into too much trouble. I'm proud of all of you. Your father would be proud of who you've become. With Brie, I just worry. She's still a girl, she works three jobs, and always keeps a good face on, but I'm not sure how hard it's really been on her." He sighed.

"Well you can see when you go to graduation, and at least get an idea of what has been going on. Why is she working three jobs? I ask her every time I talk to her or hear from her if she needs anything. Of course I never hear from her." He raked his hand in his hair.

"Well she is stubborn our Brie." Mr. Warhol smiled at him. "You probably know that better than anyone else. As for graduation, I'm not sure about all of that just yet." He glances at his wife. "We will have to see."

"You are going aren't you?" Alex sat up. "She needs you there, it's important to her."

"We are going to try that's for certain." Mr. Warhol patted his hand and stood up to refill his drink.

Alex sat back lost in thought. He smiled at Mrs. Warhol who handed him some chocolate cake. He loved the way it felt here. The house that hugs you. He smiled and they went on talking about Brandon's new baby.

The next week and a half, Alex made all of the necessary preparations for the trip. Some of those preparations included securing seats to fly to New York for not only him, but Mr. Warhol and his wife. Money was the issue, though Mr. Warhol didn't want to discuss it. Alex didn't want to give him any reason to refuse his help. He had the tickets delivered to the house and when Mr. Warhol called to complain, he said they were free with his frequent flyer miles and they were also nonrefundable. He wouldn't want to waste them would he? He didn't think Mr. Warhol bought it, but he relented and was grateful.

They were all leaving in the morning and Alex had some work to complete before he could just leave town. He worked into the night with a sense of excitement. What was wrong with him. It was a graduation not a wedding? He smiled to himself. She was going to be surprised when she saw the three of them show up. They decided to surprise her. He knew she hated surprises, but it serves her right for never writing him back, he thought. He smiled and fell asleep.

The flight was on time and Alex could only grin as he heard Mr. Warhol fuss about first class and how it just "wasn't right." Mrs. Warhol, on the other hand was in awe, and was happily sampling all the food on the flight, much to Alex's' amusement. They settled in for the flight and he drifted off.

Nothing was going right! Brienne was furious. She was pacing for more than an hour waiting to get her final grade in one of her classes. This grade would determine her GPA and ultimately be a huge factor on her resume. Not only that, she had graduation today and she wasn't even sure if her father was coming at all. She called him all morning and nothing. Nothing! She glanced at the clock and hit refresh on the computer. There it was...A.

She did it. She completed law school at the top of her class. She was Valedictorian. She swallowed and sat down. She felt the stress of the last three years melt away. It was worth it. She stood and started to dance. No one could see her. She was in her own place, so why not. She bounced around some mix of the hula and the running man. She stopped in a huff and plopped into the chair. Today was the day. The day she could start to relax.

Her father asked her to come home for a while....Alex was there. She pushed him out of her mind. He was probably married to Alice by now. She stood and gathered her things to head to the graduation.

She arrived at the stadium and was greeted by Professor Abrams who handed her the tassels to wear for the ceremony.

"Thank You." It's all she could get out. She hoped and prayed for this moment. She prepared a speech just in case. She knew the running was between her and one other person. The ceremony began. The usual lengthy pomp and circumstance, and she made a point of keeping her speech short and sweet. She focused on the importance of family and friends, and shared a story from her childhood. She felt the sweet relief of months of work as she walked across the stage and was handed her diploma.

That's when she saw him. As she walked down the aisle back to her seat, she saw his blue eyes and black hair. He was clapping for her as she walked by. He made eye contact and she felt her knees go weak. What was he doing here? She could think of nothing else as she waited for the ceremony to end. As people began to filter out, she was able to find him easily enough. He towered over most people. He had to be 6 ft. tall. His hair was still dark and slightly wavy on top now. He looked older and wiser somehow. She wasn't the only one to be taken back.

Alex stood rooted to the spot. She literally took his breath away. Gorgeous, her red flaming hair was artfully arranged around her shoulders, framing her face. She was wearing heels and a short black dress. She was older, more mature and ...perfect. He swallowed hard as she made her way over to him. She looked to his right and saw her father and his new wife.

"Daddy?" She ran to him and he engulfed her in a hug. It was obvious he was crying.

"I am so proud of you baby girl, you did it!!" He smiled widely and introduced her to his wife. They made small talk for a moment longer when Mr. Warhol cleared his throat and took his wife by the elbow.

"Dear let's make our way to the car, I believe we are going to dinner, Alex, we will meet you at the car." He gave Alex a wink and headed out.

"Hello brat." He smiled at her.

"You know I hate that Alex." She smiled at him anyway. "What are you doing here and how in the world did you find them?"

"I made them come with me on the plane, I don't like being alone. Your father doesn't take help lightly."

"No he doesn't. I tried to make some extra money to send, but he wouldn't hear of it. You can tell me how much Alex, and I'll get it back to you."

"Don't be ridiculous Brie, think of it as a graduation gift. I brought them here and I'll take them home. Almost like a role reversal from our younger years. I owe him that much. He got me out of so much trouble."

"Like Ole Sampson's window?" she glanced over at him and giggled.

"Exactly." He held the door for her leading outside to the car. He rented a car and driver and she was surprised by the limo that waited for them.

"Alex really?" she looked over at him.

"Happy graduation brat, even if you don't ever call me." He ushered her into the waiting car and they headed to dinner.

It was a happy occasion, everyone was chattering away about everything from graduation to life in Dale City. Brie told them about work and all of the cases she worked on. Eventually, Mr. Warhol announced that he was old and wanted to go back to the hotel. Not one to be disrespectful, Alex asked for the check, which he paid for, despite the protests of the dinner party. They made their way back to the hotel where Mr. and Mrs. Warhol said their goodbyes and made their way upstairs. Brienne looked at Alex. She was a little tipsy from the champagne at dinner but not so much that she wasn't aware of her surroundings.

"Want to go watch a movie in my room or something?" He asked it casually as though they were still in school, bored on a Friday night.

"Sure I don't have to go to work tonight." She giggled and Alex looked at her for a long moment. She was working in a bar of all places. She could have been hurt.

They made their way up to his room which had its own living room and she draped herself on the couch unceremoniously. He moved to make some coffee, watching her frustration with her dress being too tight to sit comfortably.

"Hey brat if you want, I have pajamas with me, you could wear them if you want to lose that dress." He froze the moment he said the words. "You know what I mean...they are on the sink in the bathroom."

Brienne made her way into the bathroom and changed. When she returned. She found him artfully arranging cups on a tray. She loved him her whole life and he never even knew she was there. She graduated today and wanted to do something crazy. She walked over to him. He was still in his suit but had lost the tie. She stood as close to him as she could and he braced himself and looked down at her.

She was too close. Something about her made all of the air in the room disappear. She had that mischievous look in her eye he knew so well. What was she up to? He turned to face her and try to figure it out but before he could ask, she threw her arms around him and pulled him down to her. She tasted like honey and champagne. He kissed her back, deeper longer. He pulled her closer to him and put his hands in her hair pulling her closer still.

She didn't know what she was feeling. He was kissing her back and her head was spinning. He was nipping at her mouth when the kiss finally broke. He looked at her with a sad look on his face.

What had she done? He was disappointed. She had crossed a line and would probably ruin their friendship. He just stood there looking at her.

"Alex, I'm so sorry. I just got carried away." She tried to sound reasonable.

"I understand Brie, you just had one too many drinks is all." He turned around to go back to making coffee. He dismissed her entirely. She had hoped...hoped for what? He would suddenly think of her as a girl and not one of his friends? She was a fool. She had to get out of here. She started for the door.

"Brie where are you going?" He saw her at the door. She wouldn't look at him.

"I can't stay Alex not now, I don't know if you can work through this or not but...I just don't know anything." She left the room and headed downstairs. Alex let her go. He called the driver and told him to take her wherever she wanted to go. What was he supposed to do? She never thought of him as anything other than a friend. Now he felt his heart all twisted up just like it had been 15 years ago. Why did she kiss him? Why now? He took a long drink of the coffee.

He sat down in the chair. Was it a game? It made no sense at all. The only thing he could do was try and figure it out.

An hour later he was still plagued with the reaction she caused in him. He buried that a long time ago and one kiss and she drags all of it back out again. It wasn't fair. He stood and grabbed his jacket and called his driver. He needed answers.

Her apartment was on the other side of town. He stood in front of her door and knocked. When she opened the door, he could only stare at her. Still in his pajamas, she braided her hair and washed her face. She looked just like she did years ago, all braids and freckles. She blinked and he shook his head.

"Listen brat I'm not 13 anymore. I don't know what's going on with you but we need to figure it out because I'm all twisted up all over again. He frowned because this was not what he planned to say.

"Thirteen, Alex? What are you talking about? At that age, I was following you around and you didn't even know I existed." She crossed her arms and continued. "I knew all about the bet at the dance and how you all planned to keep me from becoming a girl and all that, Mary

Jenkins told me. It's ok, I understand. I've had the crush so long I just got overly excited and kissed you, that's all."

He stood there. Bet? What the hell was she talking about and she had a crush?

"First of all there was no bet, Mary Jenkins liked me and told you that to keep us apart. I was half in love with you already then and you just went into tomboy mode as soon as we got there."

He sat down on her couch and she followed. They both sat and thought about it for a while.

"You loved me then?" she whispered it.

"I have always loved you brat." He looked at her.

"I've loved you too Alex, I just wanted you to be happy and you deserved something, someone better." She shrugged.

"There is no one better Brie, this whole time I thought you just saw me as your friend, and I had no idea." He put his hand over hers.

"I thought the same thing Alex." She looked up at him and he smiled before leaning in for another kiss.

This time is was longer deeper and meant more, it held a promise of a future where they could both be less lonely and find happiness and peace. When they separated, Alex began to chuckle.

"What's so funny, mister?" She frowned.

"I think we owe Brandon 6 bucks." They both started laughing and he pulled her into his arms again, this time for good.

****

The Billionaire's Caregiver

People often think a new beginning is something that happens when there is a tragedy. Shelby Watson, on the other hand, disagrees entirely. Sometimes, a new beginning can simply happen to someone, and not be some epiphany out of the ashes of what was once a mess.

Simply put, life happens, but starting over is never easy. Shelby sighed and stretched out her legs on the sofa. Tomorrow, she would start again. Never one to be defeated, she knew she could pull herself out of this "new mess" she was in.

There was something about the way her big toe poked through the worn socks that made her rethink that idea entirely.

"You and me, Dobbs...she scooped up her puppy who had buried its head under the thick blanket. "All we really need is each other." Dobbs was a Chihuahua mix. Shelby found him by the door of her apartment one day, and when she opened her apartment door, he ran right in.

He had been there since. It may have been the forlorn look he had about him that Shelby found endearing, or just the fact that he was standing there soaked to the bone. Whatever it was, Shelby knew she couldn't leave him out there, so she let him stay.

The sound of banging caused Shelby to wince slightly. The pipes in this old building were always making some awful noise whenever someone was taking a shower. Shelby looked around at her efficiency apartment.

Clean and tidy, it was her home. She lived in the 3rd block of town. The lower the number indicated the worse sections of town. This was no exception. Her neighbors all consisted of drug dealers and prostitutes, though none unfriendly. Shelby would work early mornings and try to be home before dark. As long as she kept to herself nothing bad would happen to her...well less likely to, anyway.

All of the details of her life had changed now. The part-time morning job she had been able to find, she had lost. Nothing of her doing, simply a cut in positions at the senior home she was working at. They had pulled her aside that morning and given her the bad news.

"Shelby, your work here has always been wonderful. I hope you realize this is not a reflection on the quality of your work. It's simply based on the financial needs of the company." Dr. Brenner sighed and looked over at her as he delivered the news.

"Many of the seniors are moving into better equipped facilities and they...well they already have staff there. He ran his thin bony fingers through is even thinner hair.

It was obvious to Shelby this wasn't something he enjoyed doing and decided to help take the pressure off.

"I understand Dr. Brenner. I really do. I just don't know how I'm going to make it now." Life had always been a series of ups and downs for Shelby, and this was just one more set back. She stood to stand and extended her hand to Dr. Brenner.

"Thank you for helping me get things going here, Dr. Brenner. The last three years have been wonderful. I hope you will let me use you for a reference." He stood and methodically pumped her hand, covering the hands with his other one.

"I really am sorry, Shelby."

There was a sense of helplessness that Shelby felt when she headed home. Now, she and her pup gracefully sat on the old worn sofa she had gotten from the thrift store down the street. Shelby decided it was time to start sorting the factors of her life out. She jumped up and grabbed her notebook from the counter.

Determined, she created her spreadsheet, lists of bills, things to do, what not to do, etc. Balancing her checkbook, Shelby calculated that she was okay for the next three weeks, but when the rent was due, she would be in trouble. She walked into her kitchen and pulled some canned spaghetti from the cupboard, methodically it them in a bowl and then the microwave.

This is not where she envisioned herself a few years ago. She had big plans to go back to college to get her graduate degree in nursing. She was barely scraping by, but she knew that her resilience was powerful and that she would make it through. The one thing she was sure of was that she would not cry about it but would just keep moving on.

The next day, things seemed bleak. Shelby walked to the corner store and bought a newspaper and began sifting through the want ads looking for a job. She wasn't above doing anything, and would do whatever necessary to keep things going. Sitting on her foot, she took notice of anything related to her field first.

Under the dark header, she saw an ad for a home health nurse. Perfect. She picked up the phone and called, but was greeted by a nasty voice.

"Kayla I told you I can't do this with you right now. You will just have to trust me. It's better this way." Shelby winced at the explosion.

"I'm sorry, Sir. I think I may have the wrong number, I was calling about an ad." As she began to cradle the phone back into the receiver, she heard him yell.

"Wait yes, Oh God, I'm an idiot. Miss...Miss?" He was obviously flustered.

"I'm here."

"Good. I'm terribly sorry. Your number was just like someone else's, and well... Okay, so yes, can you come out today? I need to wrap this up before I leave this weekend, and I have only gotten a few responses."

Encouraged, Shelby shot up out of her chair. "Yes, of course I can, what time?"

"Um, let me think." She heard shuffling on the other end. "How about now?"

"Now?" Shelby looked around mentally, figuring out what to wear." Sure, now is good. I just need an address."

After getting all the necessary information, Shelby changed into a light grey dress and black boots. She pulled her hair back and gathered up all of her references. As she started to walk out, she grabbed her purse and said a silent prayer.

"Wish me luck Dobbs, this is for dinner tonight."

Maneuvering her car down the highway was easy. Shelby loved road trips and had been into the town of Fauquier many times. Often considered the "rich" area, she never had much opportunity or reason to come this far out before.

Today was different. She had an interview, and hoped it would fix this mess she was in. Pulling down the long winding road into the countryside, Shelby admired the houses as she passed them. Most of them were old, and laced with gingerbread latticework. They looked warm and cozy. At the end of one street in particular, Shelby found the house she was looking for.

All she could do was stop the car and look up in awe. There is no way, she thought to herself. The magnificent mansion was on top of a ridge high above the roadway. There was a winding back entrance that was gated, and the front lawn was landscaped perfectly. Shelby glanced over at her car with it's rusted out fenders, and wondered if she really knew what she was doing.

With a sigh, she pushed her glasses back up and drove up the driveway. She pulled off to one side, straightening her dress as she stood and shut the door. She mentally prepared herself for whatever was on the other side of the door, took a deep breath, and knocked.

Billionaire, Michael had never been more frustrated in his life. He was handling the merger of two companies, trying to line up a meeting with his partner, and simultaneously trying to find someone who could care for his grandmother. At 40, Michael was all business, with dark hair and eyes and didn't have time for anything frivolous. His grandmother was his only soft spot. She raised him, and her encouragement is what created the man he was now.

Suddenly ill, the doctors believed she had a stroke, and now she was in bed and unwilling to do anything. He glanced over at the clock. Where was this girl anyway? She seemed interested, but was probably another "no show." He started gathering up some paperwork just as there was a knock at the door.

Shelby waited patiently. When the door finally did open, she found herself stunned for a moment as she looked at the most handsome man she had ever met. Tall and dark, he was almost like a sculpture. Trying not to stare, she attempted to recover quickly.

"Hello, I'm Shelby. We spoke on the phone." She held out her hand to him.

Michael took her hand, shaking it lightly. He was not without his own reaction to her. Small and petite, she had hair piled on top of her head. It was dark brown and a wonderful accent to her almond-colored eyes. She wore little makeup, and was a natural beauty.

"I'm glad you're here, though I thought you would have been here sooner." Shelby frowned at the gruffness in his voice. He wasn't as pleasant as she had hoped.

"I'm sorry, I was coming from Manassas." She tried not to take offense, as he was obviously very busy.

"I see. I am looking for someone to care for my grandmother. Full-time and an occasional Saturday. I try to be here on weekends as often as I can, and she has another nurse as well. I need someone who can try to get her to do more, or at least want to. She had a stroke a month ago and the doctors think she should be fine to get out again, but she is simply laying there." He paused to look her over.

"You're very small. Are you sure this is something you'd be interested in?"

Shelby felt the anger rise. "Mr. Jameson, I can assure you that I am very capable, despite your opinion of my small stature. Would it be possible for me to meet your grandmother? I think it's always important to see how well I click with someone."

"Sure that's fine. She knows you're coming. We can head upstairs in just a few moments. I'd like to ask a few more questions first, if that's ok?"

"Certainly." Shelby relaxed slightly. The fact that this guy was an ass made the fact that he was gorgeous much easier to look past.

"Ok so I see you are working with Everest Healthcare. Do you plan to continue to do that as well?"

"If so, this may be a bad idea. I really need 100% attention for this. My grandmother is very important to me, and multitasking is something most people think they are good at, but sadly..." he looked her over once again, "are not."

Fuming, Shelby responded in clipped tones. "No, I am no longer there. I was let go recently." Before she could elaborate, Michael interjected quickly.

"Why? Was there some sort of horseplay or something? I won't tolerate any of that at all, Miss Watson. I simply won't. You do seem rather young, and I can understand if this is something that you don't feel you can handle."

He stood up as if he was dismissing her entirely.

Panic set in but even that wasn't enough to calm her anger. "Mr. Jameson, I have been working at this for a long time. I am not young, as you so nicely put it, and as a matter of fact, I'm 33. I love this type of work, and the reason I was let go was for budget cuts, not horseplay. Perhaps if you allowed people to answer your questions without simply writing them off, you would have more candidates for this position."

Shelby stood to leave.

Fire and ice. That was all he could think of. She was absolutely adorable when she was mad. He could see how her nose slightly turned red as she had been giving him a piece of her mind and although not used to being talked to like that, he gained a new kind of respect for her.

"Point taken, Miss Watson. Shall we go meet my grandmother?" He held the door to the hallway for her and allowed her to pass as he made his way up the stairs motioning for her to follow. Shelby was surprised she had even gotten this far. He was a real piece of work, this guy. Money did that to people, she thought, and could only assume that was it. Along the hallway there was artwork. Some bright, some dull, and some muted. It was a lot to take in. As they rounded the top of the stairs, Shelby looked down and couldn't help but think that her meager apartment would fit in the foyer below.

Nancy Jameson was in good spirits. She wanted to do more, but her body just wouldn't allow her to. Besides, when she is here like this, Michael comes around more. He was her only grandson and always had been her favorite.

She had three granddaughters, but they all had their own families, and were too busy to ever visit. Michael had always been special. He had dark coloring like his grandfather and was just as stubborn. She smiled warmly as Michael entered the room with a petite brunette in tow.

Nancy didn't miss the sparks that flew from the young lady's eyes as Michael made some comment on how he could show her how to use the elevator if need be.

"Grandmother this is ...I'm sorry what your name was again?" He did look guilty so Shelby took pity on him and extended her hand to Nancy.

"Hello my name is Shelby, how are you?"

"Well I'm in this bed deary so not very good, I suppose." She winked at Shelby and smiled wide.

"My grandson feels like he needs to find someone to watch over me and make me do things I am not ready to do. I suppose that's why you're here my dear. Come over here and let me get a look at you."

Having taken an immediate liking to Grandmother Nancy, Shelby complied and walked over towards the bed. Nancy noticed how her grandson followed Shelby's every move. This was interesting indeed and was exactly the distraction she needed!

After a while of discussion and rules, Shelby stood to leave. "It was very nice to meet you Miss Jameson."

"Now Dear, if you're going to be here with me all the time, I insist you call me Nancy or Grandmother, whatever suits you."

"Grandmother, no one has offered Miss Watson a job yet. I hardly think she needs to start calling you Grandmother." Michael chuckled.

"Michael Dear, it is my money is it not?" Grandmother smiled up at him lovingly and patted his hand on the bed. "So, I say she is hired."

"Shelby that is if you will take the job of course."

Never a person to have nothing to say, it took everything Shelby had not to laugh at the interplay. It would seem that Grandmother Nancy was the only one to bring Michael down a peg or two. If for that reason alone, Shelby would take the job.

"I would love to Nancy." Shelby smiled up at Nancy and then at Michael.

There was some mix of being irritated by his grandmother's words and being floored by the smile that Shelby gave him. He didn't know what to say. After clearing his throat, he kissed his grandmother on the head and turned to leave.

"Miss Watson, if you will kindly follow me back down stairs, we can go over pay and hours, and so on."

Shelby said her goodbyes again and followed Michael down the stairs. He even smelled good, like leather and soap. What was most adorable was the way his hair curled in the back of his neck just slightly. What in the world was wrong with her?

Never suckered in by the connection between men and women, she usually had a fairly good grasp on self-control. Sure she had met a few nice guys and done her share of dating, but that was a long time ago and there had been no one in at least three years. Maybe that was it, she needed to get out more.

Offering her a chair, Michael detailed the terms and pay of the job. More money than she could imagine, Shelby sat stunned while he rambled on.

"Miss Watson is that acceptable?" She glanced up at him sharply. Oh no, what had she missed.

"Yes of course, that's more than fair."

"When can you start?" He watched her closely. He could almost watch the play of emotions she was thinking and feeling.

"Anytime is fine. I don't live far, even if I was late today. So I am free anytime."

"I'm not sure if you realize that this job is more than just being here from one time to another. Obviously, you will have to move in here, as that is part of the deal." He moved to gather up his things and glanced at his watch. He was already late and was starting to get irritated, as this matter should have been handled over an hour ago.

"Oh no, I can't do that Mr. Jameson, I have my own place. I'll stay there." He was surprised. He had seen the worn shoes she was wearing, and heard the racket her poor car made as it climbed the hill to the house. He just assumed that she would be more than happy to move in.

"Suit yourself, but I may need you sleep over on occasion. Is that fair?" He caught her eye again and reached out to shake her hand.

He was all business and it suited him. She reached out and felt the warmth as he took her hand in his. She felt like he lingered perhaps just a second longer than normal; but it was probably just her imagination. There was something powerful about the way he carried himself. Like right now, just staring at her. Closing her eyes for a moment, she managed to get out "Of course."

After saying their goodbyes, Shelby made her way to the car and headed home. What was it about Michael Jameson that made her crazy? He was arrogant, stubborn and bossy. He was also handsome, loving to his grandmother, and made her feel safe. All of that from one visit. Thankfully, he didn't live in the house year round, or she would be in trouble for sure.

The next few months were a flurry of activity. Shelby commuted every day to her job with Nancy which she loved, and had enough money to pay up her rent for a while. Michael and she spoke on the phone almost every day discussing Grandmother's day and how things were going. He typically had a joke to tell, but on some days, he was distant and moody.

Either way, they had come a long way and she considered him a friend. Gone was the canned spaghetti, and Shelby was actually able to cook food for herself. Even Dobbs was happier. She had just settled down to watch TV for a bit before turning in when the phone rang. It was a frantic Michael.

"Watson, my grandmother seems to have had a heart situation of some kind. I am in town and headed to the hospital and she has asked to see you." He was obviously in pain as he choked it out. Despite their differences, Michael had been nothing but nice with her and she didn't want to see him hurt. Worry was a motivator for Shelby and she immediately started to change clothes as he talked.

"..wanted to know if she had been acting differently lately or anything?"

"No no, she's been fine, and we have actually been walking a few times and..."

He cut her off immediately. "You had her walking? What in the world, Watson were you thinking? She wasn't ready for that. Just come to the hospital as soon as you can." He hung up leaving Shelby stunned.

She was frustrated herself wondering if he was right. She gathered up her purse and headed downstairs. Trying to avoid the people in the halls, she made it to her car safely and let out a deep sigh. Unfortunately, it was not meant to be. As she turned the key nothing happened. Slowly, she laid her head on the steering wheel. What now? She jumped out to look under the hood. Apparently, sometime during the night, someone had stolen her battery... now she was stuck. Knowing she could never forgive herself if she didn't see Nancy, Shelby made her way back to her apartment and called him.

"Yes What!" He yelled into the phone.

"Michael, please don't yell at me."

"Oh it's you. I'm sorry, Watson. The number thing again. Yes what's up?"

After much explaining, it was settled that Michael would come by and pick Shelby up on his way. She wasn't too far from the hospital herself but at night it was better to ride with someone. A few minutes later Shelby heard the knock on her door and opened it to a disheveled Michael. He was a mess, worry etched on his face, but handsome as ever.

Michael took in the apartment, if that's what you call it. Small but tidy, he imagined she could do just about everything. His issue was with her neighbors.

"This..is where you live, Shelby?" He gestured to the occupants sitting in the halls and the loud music.

"Yes why?" Shelby had her pride. This was her place and it wouldn't sit well if he was insulting.

"I'm terrified for my safety out there. I can't imagine how you've made it all this time. You're so small and there are at least 20 people just hanging outside."

"I am not so small and I am just fine. Let's go." She crammed her gloves into her purse and yanked open the door leaving it open so he could follow.

In the car Michael looked over at her. She had her signature bun in place and there was a pained look on her face. Obviously, he had hurt her feelings.

"Look Watson, I'm sorry. I didn't mean anything by it. I just worry. I mean grandmother worries about you is all." She had noticed the slip he made and smiled inwardly. He cared.

They arrived at the hospital and Nancy looked tired, but was noticeably happy to see her two favorite people. These two sure move slowly and I'm not getting any younger, she thought. She smiled at them both. What a striking couple they make. This little heart "issue" was just what was needed to bring them together for a while.

"Oh my dears, I'm so happy to see you both. They say I'm ok but are keeping me for a few days for observation. Can you imagine two whole days? I'll be bored out of my mind." Truthfully, she was glad. She had been feeling uncomfortable today but she knew Michael was coming to town and wanted he and Shelby to spend some time together.

"I'm just glad you're okay." Shelby was concerned at how pale she was. "This is my fault. We shouldn't have been walking this week."

"Oh pish posh. It's probably just gas or something." Michael rolled his eyes at his grandmother.

It was at that time that the nurse came in.

"I'm sorry, but you'll both have to get going Mrs. Jameson need to rest..."

They said their goodbyes and headed out front. Michael was very quiet, brooding again over some business merger gone wrong or something. She glanced over at him and he was caught up in thought, so she let the ride continue on in silence.

They pulled into her apartment complex and Shelby began to open the door.

"Wait, Watson I'm going up with you. I need to make sure you get in there in one piece."

"You don't have to do that Michael, I'm fine." She started walking and he followed anyway.

As they reached the top stairs of the building, a man reached over and touched Shelby on her leg making her jump. Michael immediately jumped.

"Don't touch her!" he moved between Shelby and the man.

"Michael it's fine. He is harmless." Secretly, she was touched that he jumped to her rescue.

Opening the door, they went inside. Michael was again impressed by the simple charm of her place. He sat down on the sofa and was greeted by a flying ball of fur. "Oh my, what is this?" He scruffed the dog on the back of the head and it bounced off.

"You once told me you had a dog but I hardly think that little thing qualifies, Watson." He smiled up at her.

Shelby had moved to the other end of the couch. "He is something, that's for sure." She giggled as they watched him get into a fight with a dog toy.

"You should just move into the house with us, Shelby." Hearing these words, Shelby caught her breath. She even noticed he had used her first name.

"Why would I do that? I'm perfectly fine here." What she didn't say was that she couldn't handle watching him with the various women he dated. She cared too much about Grandmother Nancy to ruin her relationship by being too close to him."

At that moment there was an obvious gunshot. Michael jumped up, and in his demanding voice she had grown to love he simply stated, "Get some things, Watson you're going with me."

The ride to the house was uneventful. Shelby knew he was mad, but to be honest, she wasn't sure why. He parked his car in front of the house and they went inside together. "You can have the room down here. I'll sleep upstairs and you know your way around, I'm getting a drink, I certainly need it."

She could use one herself, she thought as she went into the spare room downstairs. Changing into pajamas, letting her hair down, and tucking Dobbs into the bed, Shelby decided to go into the den where Michael was and get that drink. If, for any other reason but to calm her nerves. Knowing they were here alone was setting her on edge.

He was sitting in the leather-bound chair by the fireplace. He already had a drink, or was it two? Nothing could prepare him for her entrance. It felt like someone had punched him in the stomach. She was in all pink and her hair was flowing down her back. This casual image of her was one he had played out in his mind during one of their conversations on the phone. He had thought about it ...and now here it was.

He watched her walk over to the bar, pour a drink for herself, and tip it back. Impressive he thought. He stood up and moved closer to her. He could see all the shades of auburn in her hair when he was up close like this, she smelled like honeysuckle.

"You're moving in here, Watson." He said it with a finality that only made her angry.

"You can't tell me what to do, Michael. I work for you, but you don't own me." She was flushed with anger as he turned towards her.

"You could be killed, Watson. That place is dangerous, men groping you in the halls and gunshot...real actual gunshot, Watson." He ran his hand though his hair.

"My grandmother would kill me if anything happened to you and I didn't try and stop it." She couldn't help but feel some disappointment at the words. She had hoped he would say something about how he cared.

"I'm not moving in Michael. Let it go." She put her glass down and turned to leave. He grabbed her left arm and spun her around. It could have been the alcohol or the stress of the day, but something made him lose himself in that moment.

He gripped her wrist tighter than he meant to and put his right hand into the waves of her hair, pulling her towards him. The kiss had meant to be angry. He needed her to listen to reason but what started out hard, became softer, deeper, and more meaningful. Slowly, he dropped her other wrist and cupped her face in his hands, nipping at her lips and taking in the smell of her skin. When the kiss broke, he looked up at her.

"Watson, you're driving me crazy." He dropped his hands back down and watched the emotions play out on her face. Rocked to her core, Shelby could only stand and wait. Wait for the fluttering to subside, wait for her heart to stop racing, and wait for him to stop looking at her so intently. Not knowing what to say, she turned and walked stiffly back into her room. He followed her.

"Talk to me Watson. Why are you running from me? I know you feel this craziness just like I do."

"Yes I do Michael and that's why I won't live here." She turned to look at him. "I am a mess inside and I need you to go and leave me be so I can think straight." She saw the pained look on his face but heard him leave the room.

Shelby laid in bed thinking about that kiss. His kiss only intensified the connection they had. It wasn't all her. That was comforting, but what wasn't, was that she couldn't stop the fluttering she felt deep down. The way he moved towards her and the way he kissed deeply and without thought.

Laying here was obviously not going to figure it all out. She decided to go get a drink of water. They came from such different worlds. He always had someone worldly on his arm, some debutante. She had even met a few of them when he was there and she had been working.

The one thing they all had in common was that they were beautiful. Always regal and gorgeous, she always found something to do to keep away from them. After they would leave, Grandmother Nancy always had some snide comment about each one that made Shelby giggle.

"He will never find the right one unless he shops from a different field," she would say. Smiling now, Shelby opened the refrigerator door and started sifting through things until she found exactly what she wanted. Cake, it was the best cake around and had been left over from a party Grandmother Nancy had earlier that week. She stood there eating quietly, not hearing him until he spoke.

"You have quite the "strictly business" thing going on here, Watson."

She slammed the door shut on impulse, having been caught red handed.

"Yeah I try." She smiled slightly. He walked over to her and with one finger, wiped the chocolate off her bottom lip.

Feeling the heat begin to creep up again, Shelby took a step back.

"We need to talk Watson, and now." He walked until she had backed up to the bar. He moved his face closer to hers.

"I think it's obvious that I want you. I don't know how else to put it." The bluntness of the statement made Shelby gasp.

"The only way I'm going to stop trying is if you tell me you don't feel the same way." She was pinned between him and the bar and he was watching her face.

"Michael let me go," she tried to squirm but it was no use. She was stuck.

"Just tell me you don't want me to touch you and I'll leave you alone Watson. Just say it."

Knowing full well she felt the same way he did she, Shelby did the only thing she thought was right. She looked up at him and ran her finger down the right side of his face.

"I can't tell you any of that, Michael because I want the same thing." Before she could finish the words, he crushed his mouth to hers. He put his hands in her hair tilting her head back more. She kissed him back more fervently, having let go now. He lifted her up off the floor and put her on the bar top. Running his hands along her legs, all the while teasing and nipping her bottom lip.

"We should stop Michael." It was more of a pant than a statement.

"You're right, Watson, we should, but I can't. Not anymore." Pulling her to him, he lifted and carried her into the bedroom and kicked the door shut behind him. Sitting her down, she stood motionless, watching him take his shirt off and move towards her. She was frozen to the spot she stood on, not knowing what to do next.

He walked to her and started slowly unbuttoning the front of her pajamas. Each button exposed new skin that he had to kiss. He loved the way she smelled of sunshine and honeysuckle. He looked up at her.

Needing no words, she walked backwards towards the bed, pulling him with her as they went. Sliding back onto the comforter, he followed, pressing the length of him against her body. He looked down and knew in that moment, he was lost. Her hair spilled across the pillow, her lips were parted slightly from being thoroughly kissed, and her eyes were shining up at him. He could tell she was scared and excited. He ran his finger along her bottom lip.

"I need to hear you say it, Shelby. I need us to be real in this moment and together."

He gazed at her. "I can stop if you want, but you need to tell me now before I can't anymore." His honestly made her want him even more. She slowly pulled her shirt off and tossed it to the floor.

"I want you Michael, I always have." Needing no further encouragement, Michael stood and took off the rest of his clothes looking down. He stood back for a moment, letting himself take in her naked form. She was perfect.

Once, he thought her tiny, but looking at her now, he could see every curve she was given. Almost scared to touch her, she made the move first.

"I'm getting a little self-conscious Michael. What's wrong with me?" She started to cover up again.

"No don't "...he grabbed her hand. "You're beautiful, Watson, absolutely beautiful." He laid down on the bed again, taking a moment to calm his racing heart. He was acting like a teenage school boy, wondering why in the world was so nervous.

This was different. He knew it and probably always had, but he needed her to feel loved, wanted, and cherished.

The night progressed, and the two made love into the early hours of dawn. Before falling asleep, the last thing she heard was him saying her name and draping one arm across her body. Sometime during the night, Shelby got cold, having been woken up by something, only to find herself naked as the day she was born. She tried to keep from moving, but right before she almost fell asleep, she felt Michael's arm grasp her stomach and pull her into him. He kissed her ear and they drifted back to sleep for a few more hours.

Never a late sleeper, Michael woke up to greet the day with a smile on his face. Shelby was amazing. She was not just beautiful, she was the type of woman men dream of. She gave as much as she received, and never held back. This was something Michael couldn't help but admire. He looked at her lying among the sheets as he headed upstairs to shower and get ready for the day. He just didn't have the heart to wake her up.

Shelby woke up to the smells of coffee and the clink of pans. She rolled over to snuggle in more and her eyes flew open as she remembered...everything. Oh wow she had never been so careless in her life. She scrambled to jump in the shower before he found her. Before she was soaped up she heard him come into the bathroom.

"Watson, I see you're joining me today finally." He chuckled.

"Michael really, I am in the shower, I'll be right out." She could only smile as she heard him hum a tune as he left.

What would she do now? It had happened and there was no going back, but she could stop it now. Now that they had gotten it out of their system, she could put Michael Jameson out of her mind altogether.

She entered the kitchen, dressed for the day and ready to go to the hospital. Michael was cheery and leaned towards her as if to get a kiss. She managed to avoid it discretely.

Frowning, Michael went back to cooking. Something was wrong. Breakfast passed with no mishaps and they set off for the hospital.

Grandmother was overjoyed to see them. They each took a side and listened to her tell them about how awful the night had been and the bed situation. She moved on to complain about the food and how happy she would be at home. She could tell something was amiss between the couple, but it would sort itself out.

Michael was having a hard time understanding what Shelby was thinking. The night had been something people only dream about and yet when he got close to her, she ran. Something wasn't right, but he would find out soon enough.

The doctors came in and discussed the grandmother's situation. They equated it to a chemical reaction to something she ate, at which grandmother smiled. They passed the morning laughing with her, planning the next event. At lunch, the doctors ordered them out, saying she needed her rest, so the couple decided to go to a nearby restaurant for something to eat.

It was a beautiful café, overlooking a pond and situated amongst lush landscaping. They dined on wine and oysters, which were new to Shelby. Michael was about to broach the subject plaguing him, when a woman came up to the table.

"Michael darling, where have you been?" The woman was like something from the cover of a magazine. She had on long flowing pants and a silk shirt complete with a huge brimmed hat.

"Baby, I have missed you so much. How nice of you to bring the maid to lunch." She smiled over at Shelby, who immediately excused herself and went outside.

Angry Michael pushed the woman back away from him. "I told you to leave me alone. Why are you here? Stop calling me and stop following me."

Without waiting for an answer, he stormed out onto the street and to his car. Shelby was standing by the passenger side and he opened the door, then went to his side and got in.

"I'm sorry, Watson that was ...the number..." at her confused look he added "remember when you would call and I thought it was her?"

"Aha that is her." Shelby still felt awful about the exchange and self-conscious as well. The maid, really?

When they arrived at the house, Shelby went to her room. Thinking she would have some time to think, she was surprised when Michael stormed in behind her.

"What the hell Shelby, after last night I thought,"

"What...you thought we would just act like nothing happened? You think I would go away? Well I'm not. I love Grandmother Nancy and I'm not going anywhere."

"What are you talking about Shelby? I don't want you to go anywhere. I want you here. With me." He said it with such finality, Shelby could do no more than look up at him.

"What?"

"I love you Shelby. I have since the day we met and you came here. But when I was at your place and heard that gunshot it was all I could do to not kidnap you myself and tie you up here so I could keep you safe."

"But I'm not like you Michael. She called me "the maid" for goodness sake." She looked down for a moment.

"Shelby do you really think I care one moment about what people think?" I want you and I choose you."

Tears were flowing freely now as Shelby looked up at him.

"Well," He asked impatiently.

"Well what? " She was confused.

"Damn it Shelby, you're killing me. Do you or do you not feel anything for me?"

Laughing, she ran into his arms and kissed him. "Michael I have loved you from the moment you opened that door."

He let out an audible sigh. Happy and content, he pulled her close to him and kissed her deeply.

Hand in hand they headed back to the hospital. Grandmother had taken a nap and was refreshed as she looked out the windows to the parking lot. Seeing Michael, she smiled. He really was a good boy. But what made her happiest was seeing him hand in hand with Shelby.

Perhaps her plan had worked after all, and if she played it just right, she could somehow start planning a Fall wedding at the house. She may be getting old, but this was enough to keep her busy for many more years to come.

****

About the Author

J.L. Ryan is a bestselling author who has written over 50 books, including the wildly popular Billionaire Boys Club, Billionaire Games, Billionaire Bachelors, and Adventures In Romance. Ryan has also attended numerous book signings and writer's conventions including Romance Writers Of America Conferences. Living in New York, J.L. enjoys spending time with family and friends, volunteering at a large metropolitan homeless shelter, and working in the dog rescue community.